Reprint Publishing

FOR PEOPLE WHO GO FOR ORIGINALS.

www.reprintpublishing.com

John Kendrick Bangs

Over the Plum-Pudding

by

John Kendrick Bangs

Author of

"A House-Boat on the Styx"
"Coffee and Repartee"
"The Idiot at Home"
"The Idiot"

Illustrated

New York and London
Harper & Brothers Publishers
1901

TO

JOHN KENDRICK BANGS, Jr.

WHOSE FONDNESS FOR PLUM PUDDINGS

SUGGESTS THE PROPRIETY OF THIS

𝔇𝔢𝔡𝔦𝔠𝔞𝔱𝔦𝔬𝔫

Thanks are due to the Publishers of *Harper's Round Table*, *Harper's Weekly*, *The Delineator*, *Life*, *Brooklyn Life*, and the New York *Mail and Express* for permission to republish these stories in collected form.

Contents

Illustrations

Illustrations

"Over the Plum-Pudding"

WHY IT WAS NEVER PUBLISHED. AN AUTHORITATIVE STATEMENT BY ITS EDITOR.

On the eve of his departure for Manila, where he is shortly to begin the publication of a comic paper, my friend Mr. Horace Wilkinson, late literary adviser of Messrs. Hawkins, Wilkes & Speedway, the publishers, sent to me the following pages of manuscript with the request that I should have them published for the benefit of those whom the story may concern. I have cheerfully accepted the commission, desiring it to be distinctly understood, however, that I am in no sense responsible for Mr. Wilkinson's statements, either of fact or of opinion. I am merely the medium through whom his explanation is brought to the public eye.

J. K. B.

"Over the Plum-Pudding"

I

I HAVE been asked so often and by so many persons known and unknown to me why it was that a Christmas book that was to have been issued some years ago under my editorial supervision never appeared, although announced as ready for immediate publication, that I feel that I should make some statement in explanation of the seeming deception. The matter was very annoying, both to my publishers and to myself at the time it happened, and while I was anxious then to make public a full and candid statement of the facts as they occurred, Messrs. Hawkins, Wilkes & Speedway deemed it the wiser course to let the affair rest for a year or two anyhow. They failed to see my point of view, that, while they were responsible for the advertisement, I was

3

"Over the Plum-Pudding"

assumed to be responsible for the book, and in the event of its failure to appear it would naturally be inferred by the public that my work had not proven sufficiently up to standard to warrant them in continuing the venture. I did not press the matter, however, being too busy on other affairs to give to it the attention it deserved, and until now no opportunity to explain my connection with the unfortunate volume has arisen. I should hesitate even at this late date to give a wide publicity to the incident were it not that my mail has lately been overburdened by rather peremptory requests from the several contributors to the volume to be informed what had become of the tales they wrote and for which they were to be paid on publication. Ordinarily, letters of this kind I should refer to my business principals, the publishers themselves, but in this emergency it happens, unfortunately for me, that the publishers have been retired from business and are now engaged in other pursuits: one of them at the Klondike, another as a veterinary surgeon - general at Santiago, on the appointment of the Secretary of War, and

the third living somewhere abroad *incog.*
as the result of his having drawn out all
the capital of his partners and fled one
early spring morning two years ago, leaving behind him his best wishes and about
eight thousand dollars in debts for his
partners to pay. It therefore devolves on
me to explain to the irate authors as best
I can what happened. The explanation
may not be shirked, for they are wholly
within their rights in demanding it. My
only hope is that they will be satisfied with
my statement, although I am quite conscious, sadly so, of the fact that to certain
suspicious minds it may seem to lack cred-
ibility.

II

To begin, I will place the responsibility
for the whole affair where it belongs. It
was the fault of no less a person than Mr.
Rudyard Kipling. Mr. Andrew Lang's
connection with the episode, of course, involved us in the final catastrophe, but he
is not to blame. Mr. Kipling started the
whole affair, and if Mulvaney and Ortheris

and Learoyd had behaved themselves properly the book would now be resting calmly upon many an appreciative library shelf, instead of being, as it is, but a sorrowful memory and a possible cause for a series of international lawsuits.

This fact being understood as the basis of my argument, I will proceed to prove it; and to do so properly I must give in brief outline some idea of the contents of the book. It was to be called "Over the Plum-Pudding; or, Tales Told Under the Mistletoe, by Sundry Tattlers. Edited by Horace Wilkinson"—in fact, I hold a copyright at this moment upon this alluring title. Furthermore, it was to be unique among modern publications in that, while professing to be a Christmas book, the tales were to be full of Christmas spirit. The idea struck me as a very original one. I had observed that Fourth-of-July issues of periodicals were differentiated from the Christmas numbers only in the superabundance of advertisements in the latter, and it occurred to me that a Christmas publication containing some reference to the Christmas season would strike the public as novel

"Over the Plum-Pudding"

—and, in spite of the unfortunate overturning of my schemes, I still think so. Messrs. Hawkins, Wilkes & Speedway thought so, too, and gave me *carte blanche* to go ahead, stipulating only that I should spare no expense, and that the stories should be paid for on publication. I was also to enlist the services of the best persons in letters only.

Taking this last stipulation as the basis of my editorial operations, it is not a far cry to the conclusion that I sought to get stories from such eminent writers as Mr. Hall Caine, Dr. Doyle, Mr. Kipling, Richard Harding Davis, Andrew Lang, George Meredith, and myself. There were a few others, but these were people whose light shone forth suddenly and brilliantly, and then went out. I shall have no occasion to mention their names. It is enough to call attention to the fact that ultimately they were all I had left.

Mr. Caine's contribution was a charming little fancy written originally for children, but sent to me because it was the only thing the author happened to have on hand at the moment he received my request. It

"Over the Plum-Pudding"

was called, if I remember rightly, "The Inebriate Santa Claus." It was full of that spirit of life and gayety which has been such a marked feature of Mr. Caine's work in the past, and was written with all of that fine, manly vigor that Mr. Caine puts into his every word. Sunshiny, I should call it, if I were seeking for the one word which summed up the virtues of "The Inebriate Santa Claus." One glowed as one perused it with the warmth of the whole thing, especially in such passages as this, for instance:

" His downward trip through the chimney of Marston Hall gave him confidence in himself. He had observed as he was about to leave the roof of Higginbottom Castle that his footprints in the snow were suggestive of his actual condition, and he wondered if he could possibly get through the evening's work without catastrophe. But the Marston Hall chimney flue restored his confidence. It was straight, and after his descent the soot, that clung to the inner walls like bad habits to a man, showed none of the vacillating lines which were the essential characteristic of his footprints on the roof. He was sobering up."

I wish I could remember the story as a

whole. It would be unjust, however, to the author to try to reproduce it from memory, and I shall not make the effort. It went on to tell, however, how the good old Saint, in his unfortunate condition of inebriacy, overturned the Christmas tree at Marston Hall and set fire to the house, resulting in a slight singeing of his own person and the destruction of the Hall, together with all the inmates, a fact that so distressed the unhappy Santa Claus that at the next nursery he visited he resolved to reform and indulge no more in strong drink, although the nurse, on putting the children to bed, had departed, leaving a bottle of whiskey upon the mantel-piece—this showing Santa Claus's powers of self-control in the face of temptation.

Altogether, as I have already said, the story was full of import and sunshine, and, as may be seen from my brief and inadequate description, was possibly more fitted for children than for the adult mind.

III

Mr. Meredith's story came next, and it

"Over the Plum-Pudding"

had all of that charm which goes with the average Meredithian production. To call it dictionaryesque is not too high praise to bestow upon it. What it was about I never really gathered, although I of course read it through several times before accepting it, and perused the proofs carefully some eight or nine times. There were allusions to Santa Claus in it, however, and I therefore let it pass, feeling that to the admirers of the master's genius its message would ring out clear and crisp like the glad chimes of the Christmas morn; and it was my desire to be the bearer of glad things to all people, whether I was myself in sympathy with their literary tastes or not. I recall one page in the story—the last of all, however, which struck me as a marvel. Fotherington, whom I guessed to be the hero, is standing on top of a shot-tower in London, about to commit suicide by jumping down, when all of a sudden Santa Claus appears beside him and inquires if the tower is a chimney or not. Fotherington gives a "throat-gasping laugh" and invites Santa Claus to join him in the jump

"Over the Plum-Pudding"

and find out for himself. The author writes:

"At this, the spirit of the Hourgod, the multitudinous larvæ of his emotions, intensified by the nose - whirling impertinence of the other, gazed, eyes tear - surging, towards the reddish northern cheek of the piping East, human in its bulk, the wharf cranes rising superabundant from the umbrageous onflowing of the commerce-ridden stream, piercing the middle distance like a mine-hid vein of purest gold in the mellowing amber of approaching dawn, flying seaward, curdling in its mad pressure ever onward, soon to be lost in the vaguely infinite, beyond which, unconscious of the perils of the inspired home-coming, lies that of which homogeneous man may speculate, but never, by reason of his inflated limitations, approximate without expletion.

"'Beg pardon!' said he, with an interrogation in his inflection. 'I was not aware of the facts.' Fotherington was silent for a moment, and then, recognizing Santa Claus, a shame - surge encarnadined his cheek, and he answered, strenuously apologetic: 'This is the shot-tower. The sight of you restores me to life. I shall not again dwell upon self - destruction. Heaven bless the spirit of the hour.'

"He buried his face in the Saint's pack, and hot tears sprang forth from his vision.

"'Beg pardon again,' observed Santa Claus, drawing himself away. 'If you must weep, weep on my shoulder, not on my pack. The toys are not painted in fast colors.'

" And the two went down together."

IV

The contribution of Mr. Davis was a most excellent sketch of the inimitable Van Bibber, and told how on his way to a dance late one evening during Christmas week he encountered, snuggled in a doorway near the North River, a poor little street gamin nearly frozen to death. Van Bibber saves the child's life by removing his dress-coat and wrapping it up in it, the result being that he has to lead the cotillon at Mrs. Winchley's clad in a fur-lined over-coat. It was a tender and touching little literary gem, and was full of the fine sentiment and lofty moralizing for which this author has always been noted. Its humor may well be imagined. The little talk between Van Bibber and Travers in the dressing-room as to Van Bibber's dilemma when he realized how his impetuosity had led him into giving the boy his coat was a characteristic bit, and ran somewhat like this:

"Over the Plum-Pudding"

"'What the deuce shall I do?' he said, fanning his somewhat flushed face with the silver-backed hand-mirror. 'I can't lead the cotillon in my shirt-sleeves.'

"'No, you can't,' assented Travers with a droll smile. 'What an ass you were not to give him your fur-lined overcoat instead.'

"'It wouldn't have fitted him,' said Van Bibber, absently. 'Poor little devil.'

"'There's only one thing you can do, Van,' said Travers after a moment's pause. 'Either don't stay, or dance in your overcoat.'

"'That's two things,' retorted Van Bibber. 'Of course I've got to stay. I told Mrs. Winchley I'd lead her cotillon, and I've got to do it. Do you suppose people would say anything if I did appear in my overcoat?'

"'Not if they had any manners they wouldn't,' said Travers. 'Of course, it will be observed, but if they know anything about good form they'll keep quiet about it.'

"'Then it's settled,' Van Bibber said, quietly. 'I'll wear the fur overcoat, and to disarm all criticism I'll simply tell everybody I have a fearful cold and don't dare take it off. Come on—let's go down. It's half past one now, and Mrs. Winchley told me she wanted to begin early, so as to have it over with before break-fast.'"

V

It was my pleasure next to have a Sher-lock Holmes story from Dr. Doyle, wherein

13

"Over the Plum-Pudding"

the great detective is once more restored to
life, and through an ingenious complication
discovers himself. His sudden disappear-
ance, which was never fully explained,
did not really result in his death, but in a
concussion of the brain in his fall over the
precipice which drove all consciousness
of his real self from his mind. Found in
an unconscious condition by a band of
yodelers, he is carried by them into the
Tyrolese Alps, where, after a prolonged
illness, he regains his health, but all his
past life is a blank to him. How he sets
about ferreting out the mystery of his identity is the burden of the story, and how he
ultimately discovers that he is none other
than Sherlock Holmes by finding a diamond brooch in the gizzard of a Christmas
turkey at Nice, where he is stopping under
the name of Higgins, is vividly set forth:

"'And you have never really ascertained, Mr.
Higgins, who you are?' asked Lady Blenkinsop,
as they sat down at Mrs. Wilbraham's gorgeous table
on Christmas night.

"'No, madame,' he replied, sadly, ' but I shall
ultimately triumph. My taste in cigars is a peculiar
one, and no one else that I have ever met can smoke

with real enjoyment the kind of a cigar that I like. I am searching, step by step, in every city for a cigar dealer who makes a specialty of that brand who has recently lost a customer. Ultimately I shall find one, and then the chain of evidence will be near to its ultimate link, for it may be that I shall turn out to be that man.' "

Thus the story runs on, and the pseudo-Higgins delights his fellow-guests with the brilliance of his conversation. He eats lightly, when suddenly a flash of triumph comes into his deep-set eyes, for on cutting open the turkey gizzard the diamond brooch is disclosed. He seems about to faint, but with a strong effort of the will he regains his strength and arises.

" ' Mrs. Wilbraham,' he said, quietly and simply— ' ladies and gentlemen, I must leave you. I take the 9.10 train for London. May I be excused?'

" The eyes of the company opened wide.

" ' Why—must you really go, Mr. Higgins?' Mrs. Wilbraham queried.

" ' It is imperative,' said he. ' I am going to have myself identified. The finding of this diamond brooch in a turkey gizzard convinces me that I am Sherlock Holmes. Such a thing could happen to no other, yet I may be mistaken. I shall call at once upon a certain Dr. Watson, of London, a friend of Holmes's, who will answer the question definitely.

" And with a courteous bow to the company he left the room, his usually pale features aglow with unwonted color."

Of course, the surmise proves to be correct, and the great detective once more rejoins his former companions, restored not only to them, but to himself. It was one of the most keenly interesting studies of detective life that Dr. Doyle or any one else has ever given us, and my regret that the story is lost to the world amounts almost to a positive grief.

VI

The only other notable efforts in the book were, as I have already indicated, from the pens of Andrew Lang and Rudyard Kipling, and as the preceding stories were characteristic of their authors, so were these equally so. I have not the time to more than suggest their tenor briefly. Mr. Lang's story was one of his charming made-over fairy tales, and he unfortunately introduced that most fearsome of dragons

16

"Over the Plum-Pudding"

Fafner into it. He was held, however, in captivity, and had the situation in which Mr. Lang left him been allowed to remain undisturbed, all would have been well, and "Over the Plum-Pudding" would not have met with disaster. Mr. Kipling, however, chose to contribute a Mulvaney story, and herein lay the whole trouble. Mulvaney and his two roystering companions, Ortheris and Learoyd, start in on a Christmas spree, and they do it in their own complete fashion, and Mr. Kipling never in his life drew his characters more vividly and vigorously; but this time he did it too vigorously. The three musketeers of the British army got beyond his control, and it is the fact that when "Over the Plum-Pudding" was ready for presentation to the public they broke loose from the story in which they were supposed to be confined; went rushing and roaring, regardless of the etiquette of the situation, through every other tale in the book, found the bottle of whiskey which the nurse-maid in Mr. Caine's story had left on the mantel-piece, drained it to the dregs, and then, under the mad influence of the alcohol, *let Fafner loose.*

17

"Over the Plum-Pudding"

Their fate may easily be imagined. They were at once destroyed by the angry beast, who, after making a meal upon them, rushed like a steam-engine through the Sherlock Holmes story, swallowing its characters one and all as though they were naught but salted almonds; breathed fire upon Meredith's shot-tower until it tottered and fell, a smoking ruin; chewed up the frozen little gamin in the Van Bibber sketch; withered Van Bibber and his overcoat and his friends by one snorting blast of steam from his left nostril; and, in fact, to make a long story shorter than it might be, strewed blue ruin from title-page to *finis* of "Over the Plum-Pudding." It is the fact that on the morning set for the presentation of the edition to the public, on opening my own copy of the book there was not a character in it left alive; not a house that had not been reduced to charred timbers and ashes; not a scene that was not withered as by the flames of perdition, and where once had been a strong portrayal of a scene of happy social revels, the ballroom of Mrs. Winchley, where Van Bibber was to lead the cotillon, lay Fafner—dead. Kipling's

18

"Over the Plum-Pudding"

characters were too much for his digestion.

VII

That is the story of "Over the Plum-
Pudding." That is why it never appeared.
That is the explanation of the editor. I
admit that in some ways the explanation
seems scarcely credible, but it is in every
respect truthful, and on my return from
Manila I will prove it to all suspicious-
minded persons who may choose to doubt
it, for I can show them the copyright papers
of the book, the advertisement of its approaching publication, my contract with
Messrs. Hawkins, Wilkes and Speedway,
and a few press notices I had myself prepared for its exploitation.

I can also prove that Mr. Kipling draws
his characters so vividly and vigorously
that they stand out like real people before
us, and certainly if they can do that, there
is no reason why they should not be able
to do all that I have claimed they did do.

HORACE WILKINSON.

19

Bills, M.D.

Bills, M.D.

A CHRISTMAS GHOST I HAVE MET

I T was the usual kind of a Christmas Eve. The snow was falling with its customary noiselessness, and the world was gradually taking on a mantle of white which made it look like a very attractive wedding - cake. It was upon this occasion that Old Bills materialized in my down-town study and got me out of a very unpleasant hole. The year had not been a very profitable one for me. My last book had been a comparative failure, having sold only 118,000 copies in the first six months, so that instead of receiving $60,000 in royalties on the first of November, as I had expected, I had fallen down to something like $47,000. There was a fraction of seven or eight hundred dollars—just what it was I cannot recall. Then my securities had, for one reason or another, failed to yield the customary revenue; some thirty or forty of my houses had not rented; taxes had increased—in short, I found myself at Christmas - time, with my wife and eight children expecting to be remembered, with less than $80,000 that I could spare in the bank.

To be sure, we had all agreed that this year we should avoid extravagance, and the little madame had informed me that she would be very unhappy if I expended more than $40,000 upon her present from myself. My daughter, too, like the sweet girl that she is, said, with a considerable degree of firmness, that she would rather have a check for $10,000 than the diamond necklace I had contemplated giving her; and my eldest son had sent word from college, in definite terms, that he didn't think, in view of the hard times, he would ask for anything more than a new pair of wheelers for his drag, three hunters, a T cart, a silver chafing-dish set, and a Corot for his smoking-room.

This spirit, as I say, permeated the household—even the baby babbled of economy, and thought he could get along with ruby jackstones and a bag of cats'-eyes to play marbles with. But even thus, as the reader can see for himself, $80,000 would not go far, and I was in despair. There is no greater trial in the world than that confronting a generously disposed father who suddenly finds himself at Christmas time without the means to carry out his wishes and to provide his little ones with the gifts which their training has justified them in expecting.

I was seated alone in my office, not hav·ing the courage to go home and tell my family of the horrid state of affairs, or, rather, putting off the evil hour, for ultimately the truth would have to be told. It was growing dark. Outside I could hear the joyous hum of the busy streets; the clanging of the crowded cable-cars, going to and fro, bearing their holiday burden of bundle-laden shoppers, seemed to sound musically and to tell of peace and good-will. Even the cold, godless world of commerce seemed to warm up with the spirit of the hour. I alone was in misery, at a moment when peace and happiness and good-will were the watchwords of human-

"Over the Plum-Pudding"

ity. My distress increased every moment as I conjured up before my mind's eye the picture of the coming morn, when my children and their mother, in serene confidence that I would do the right thing by them, should find the tree bare of presents, and discover, instead of the usual array of bonds and jewels, and silver services, and horses and carriages, and rich furs, and priceless books (the baby had cut his teeth the year before on the cover of the Grolier edition of Omar Khayyam, which, at a cost of $600, I had given him, bound in ivory and gold, with carbuncles adorning the back and the title set in brilliants)—discover, instead of these, I say, mere commonplace presents possessing no intrinsic worth—why, it was appalling to think of their disappointment! To be sure, I had purchased a suit of Russian sables for madam, and had concealed a certified check for $25,000 in the pocket of the dolman, but what was that in such times, hard as they were!

And you may imagine it was all exquisitely painful to me. Then, on a sudden, I seemed not to be alone. Something appeared to materialize off in the darker corner of the study. At first I thought it was merely the filming over of my eyes with the moisture of an incipient and unshed tear, but I was soon undeceived, for the thing speedily took shape, and a rather unpleasant shape at that, although there was a radiant kindliness in its green eyes.

"Who are you?" I demanded, jumping up and staring intently at the apparition, my hair meanwhile rising slightly.

"I'm Dr. Bills," was the response, in a deep, malarial voice, as the phantom, for that is all it was, approached me. "I've come to help you out of your troubles," it added, rather genially.

"Ah? Indeed!" said I. "And may I ask how you know I am in trouble?"

"Certainly you may," said the old fellow. "We ghosts know everything."

"Then you are a ghost, eh?" I queried, although I knew mighty well at the moment I first saw him that he was nothing more, he was so transparent and misty.

"At your service," was the reply, as my unexpected visitor handed me a gelatinous-

"Over the Plum-Pudding"

looking card, upon which was engraved the following legend:

```
* * * * * * * * * * * * * * * * * * * * * * * *
*                                             *
*            U. P. BILLS, M.D.,               *
*                                             *
*         "The Spook Philanthropist."         *
*                                             *
*        Troubles Cured While You Wait.       *
*                                             *
* * * * * * * * * * * * * * * * * * * * * * * *
```

"Ah!" said I, as I read it. "You'll find me a troublesome patient, I am afraid. Do you know what my trouble is?"

"Certainly I do," said Bills. "You're a little short and your wife and children have expectations."

"Precisely," said I. "And here is Christmas on top of us and nothing for the tree except a few trifling gems and other things."

"Well, my dear fellow," said the kindly visitant, "if you'll intrust yourself to my care I'll cure you in a jiffy. There never was a case of immediate woe that I couldn't cure, but you've got to have confidence in me."

"Sort of faith cure, eh?" I smiled.

28

Bills, M. D.

"Exactly," he replied. "If you don't believe in Old Bills, Old Bills cannot relieve your distress."

"But what do you propose to do, Doctor?" I asked. "What is your course of treatment?"

"That's my business," he retorted. "You don't ask your family physician to outline his general plan to you when you summon him to treat you for gout, do you?"

"Well, I generally like to know more of him than I know of you," said I, apologetically, for I had no wish to offend him. "For instance, are you allopath, or a homœopath, or some hitherto untrodden path?"

"Something of a homœopath," he admitted.

"Then you cure trouble with trouble?" I asked, rather more pertinently, as the event showed, than I imagined.

"I cure trouble with ease," he replied glibly. "You may accept or reject my services. It's immaterial to me."

"I don't wish to seem ungrateful, Doctor," said I, seeing that the old spook was growing a trifle irritated. "I certainly most gratefully accept. What do you want me to do?"

"Go home," he said, laconically.

"But the empty tree?" I demanded.

"Will not be empty to-morrow morning," said he, and he vanished.

I locked my study door and started to walk home, first stopping at the café down-stairs and cashing a check for $60,000. I had confidence in Old Bills, but I thought I would provide against possible failure; and I had an idea that on the way up-town I might perhaps find certain little things to please, if not satisfy, the children, which could be purchased for that sum. My surmise was correct, for, while Old Bills did his work, as will soon be shown, most admirably, I had no difficulty in expending the $60,000 on simple little things really worth having, between Pine Street and Forty-second. For instance, as I passed along Union Square I discovered a superb pair of pearl hat-pins which I knew would please my second daughter, Jenny, because they were just suited to the immediate needs of the talking doll she had received from her aunt on her birthday. They were cheap

Bills, M.D.

little pins, but as I paid down the $1,800 they cost in crisp hundred dollar bills they looked so stunningly beautiful that I wondered if, after all, they mightn't prove sufficient for little Jenny's whole Christmas, if Bills should fail. Then I met poor old Hobson, who has recently met reverses. He had an opera-box for sale for $2,500, and I bought it for Martha, my third daughter, who, though only seven years old, frequently entertains her little school friends with all the manner of a woman of fashion. I felt that the opera-box would please the child, although it was not on the grand tier. I also killed two birds with one stone by taking a mortgage for $10,000 on Hobson's house, by which I not only relieved poor old Hobson's immediate necessities, but, by putting the mortgage in my son Jimmy's stocking, enriched the boy as well. So it went. By the time I reached home the $60,000 was spent, but I felt that, brought up as they had been, the children would accept the simple little things I had brought home to them in the proper spirit. They were, of course, cheap, but my little ones do not look at the material value of their

"Over the Plum-Pudding"

presents. It is the spirit which prompts the gift that appeals to them—Heaven bless 'em! I may add here, too, that my little ones did not even by their manner seem to grudge that portion of the $60,000 spent which their daddy squandered on his immediate· impulses, consisting of a nickel extra to a lad who blacked his boots, thirty cents for a cocktail at the club, and a dime to a beggar who insisted on walking up Fifth Avenue with him until he was bought off with the coin mentioned—a species of blackmail which is as intolerable as it is inevitable on all fashionable thoroughfares.

But their delight as well as my own on the following morning, when the doctor's fine work made itself manifest, was glorious to look upon. I frankly never in my life saw so magnificent a display of gifts, and I have been to a number of recent millionaire weddings, too. To begin with, the most conspicuous thing in the room was the model of a steam yacht which Old Bills had provided as the family gift to myself. It was manifest that the yacht could not be got into the house, so Bills

Bills, M.D.

had had the model sent, and with it the information that the yacht itself was ready at Cramp's yard to go into commission whenever I might wish to have it. It fairly took my breath away. Then for my wife was a rope of pearls as thick as a cable, and long enough to accommodate the entire week's wash should the laundress venture to borrow it for any such purpose. All the children were fitted out in furs; there were four gold watches for the boys, diamond tiaras and necklaces of pearls and brilliant rings for the girls. My eldest son received not only the horses and carriages and the Corot he wanted, but a superb gold-mounted toilet set, and a complete set of golf clubs, the irons being made of solid silver, the shafts of ebony, with a great glittering diamond set in the handle of each; these all in a caddy bag of sealskin, the fur shaved off. There was a charming little naphtha launch and a horseless carriage for Jimmy, and, as for the baby, it was very evident that Old Bills had a peculiarly tender spot in his ghostly makeup for children. I doubt if the finest toyshops of Paris ever held toys in greater variety or more ingenious in design. There were two armies of soldiers made of aluminum which marched and fought like real little men, a band of music at the head of each that discoursed the most stirring music, cannons that fired real shot—indeed, all the glorious panoply of war was there in miniature, lacking only blood, and I have since discovered that even this was possible, since every one of the little soldiers was so made that his head could be pulled off and his body filled with red ink. Then there was a miniature office building of superb architectural design, with little steam elevators running up and down, and throngs of busy little creatures, manipulated by some ingenious automatic arrangement, rushing hither and thither like mad, one and all seemingly engaged upon some errand of prodigious commercial import. Another delightful gift for the baby was a small opera-house, and a complete troupe of little wax prime donne, and zinc tenors, and brass barytones, with patent removable chests, within which small phonographs worked so that the little things sang like so many music-boxes,

while in the chairs and boxes and galleries
were matinée girls and their escorts and
their bonnets and their enthusiastic applause—truly I never dreamed of such magnificent things as Old Bills provided for
the occasion. He had indeed got me out of
my immediate difficulty, and when I went
to bed that night, after the happiest Christmas I had ever known, I called down the
richest blessings upon his head; and why,
indeed, should I not? We had between
$400,000 and $500,000 worth of presents in
the house, and they had not cost me a
penny, outside of the $60,000 I had spent
on the way up-town, and what could be
more conducive to one's happiness than
such a Yuletide Klondike as that?

This was many years ago, dear reader,
before the extravagant methods of the
present day crept into and somewhat poi-
soned the Christmas spirit, but from that
day to this Old Bills has never ceased to
haunt me. He has been my constant com-
panion from that glorious morning until
to-day, when I find myself telling you of
him, and, save at the beginning of every
recurring month, when I am always very

"Over the Plum-Pudding"

busy and somewhat anxious about making ends meet, his society is never irksome. Once you get used to Bills he becomes a passion, and were it not for his singular name I think I should find him a constant source of joy.

It rather dampened my ardor, I must confess, when I found that the initials of the good old doctor, U. P., stood for Un Paid, but if you can escape the chill and irksomeness of that there is no reason why the poorest of us all may not derive much real joy in life from the good things we can get through Bills.

In justice to the readers of this little tale, I should perhaps say, in conclusion, that I read it to my wife before sending it out, and she asserts that it was all a dream, because she says she never received that rope of pearls. To which I retorted that she deserved to, anyhow—but, dream or otherwise, the visitation has truly been with me for many years, and I fear the criticism of my spouse is somewhat prompted by jealousy, for she has stated in plain terms that she would rather go without Christmas than see me constantly haunted by

Bills, M.D.

Bills; but, after all, it is a common condition, and it does help one at Christmas
time in an era when the simple observance
of the season, so characteristic of the olden
time, has been superseded by a lavish expenditure which would bring ruin to the
richest of us were it not for the benign influence of Bills, M.D.

The Flunking of Watkins's Ghost

The Flunking of Watkins's Ghost

ARLEY was a Freshman at Blue Haven University, and, like many other Freshmen, had a wholesome fear of examinations. In the football - field he was courageous to the verge of foolhardiness, but when he sat in his chair in the examination-room, with a paper covered with questions before him, he was as timid as a fawn. There was no patent flying or revolving wedge method of getting him through the rush-line of Greek, nor by any known tackle could he down the half-backs of mathematics and kick the ball of his intellect through the goal-posts, on the other side of which lay the coveted land of Sophomoredom. Hence Parley, who had spent most of his time practising for his class eleven, found himself at the end of

"Over the Plum-Pudding"

his first term in a state of worry like unto
nothing he had ever known before.

"It would be tough to fail at this stage
of the game," he thought, as he reflected
upon what his father would say in the event
of his failure. "It wouldn't be so bad to
flunk later on, but for a chap to fall down at
the very beginning of his race wouldn't reflect much credit on his trainer, and I think
it very likely the governor would be mad
about it."

"Of course he would!" said a voice at
his side. "Who wouldn't?"

Parley jumped, he was so startled. Nor
was it surprising that even so cool and
physically strong a person as he should
for an instant know the sensation of fear.
If you or I should happen to be lying off in
our room before a flickering log-fire, which
furnished the only illumination, smoking
a pipe, reflecting, and all alone, I think we
would ourselves, superior beings as we are,
be startled to hear a strange voice beside us answering our unspoken thoughts.
This was exactly what had happened in
Parley's case. Now that the football season was over, he realized that too much

The Flunking of Watkins's Ghost

time had been spent on that and too little upon his studies, and conditions were all he could see in the future. This naturally made Parley very unhappy, and upon this particular night he had retired to his room to be alone until his blue spell should wear off. Several of his classmates had knocked at his door, but he had made no response, and in order further to give the impression that he was not within he had turned out his gas and table lamp, and sat pulling viciously away at his pipe, watching the flames on the hearth as they danced to and fro upon the logs, which last hissed and spluttered away as if they approved neither of the dancing flames nor of Parley himself.

Straining his eyes in the direction whence the voice had seemed to come, Parley endeavored to ascertain who had spoken, but all was as it had been before. There was no one in sight, and the Freshman settled back again in his chair.

"Humph!" he ejaculated. "Guess I must have fallen asleep and dreamed it."

"Not a bit of it," interposed the voice again. "I'm over here in the arm-chair."

"Over the Plum-Pudding"

Parley sprang to his feet and grabbed up his "banger," as the big cane he had managed to hold to the bitter end in the rush of cherished memory was called.

"Oh, you are, are you?" he cried, controlling his fear with great difficulty; and his voice would hardly come, his throat and lips had become so dry from nervousness. "And, pray, how the deuce did you get in?" he demanded, peering over into the arm-chair's capacious depths — still seeing nothing, however.

"Oh, the usual way," replied the voice— "through the door."

"That's not so," retorted Parley. "Both doors are locked, so you couldn't. Why don't you come out like a man where I can see you, and tell the truth, if you know how?"

"Can't," said the other—"that is, I *can't* come out like a *man*."

"Ah!" sneered Parley. "What are you then—a purple cow?"

"I don't know what a purple cow is," replied the voice, in sepulchral tones. "I never saw one. They didn't have 'em in my day, only plain brown ones — cows of the primary colors."

44

The Flunking of Watkins's Ghost

"Ah?" said Parley, smartly. The invisible thing was speaking so meekly that his momentary terror was passing away: "You had blue cows in your day, eh?"

"Oh, my, yes!" replied the strange visitor; "lots of 'em. Take any old cow and deprive her of her calf, and she becomes as blue as indigo."

Here the voice laughed, and Parley joined.

"You're a clever—ah—what?—A clever It," he said.

"You might call me an It if you wanted to," said the stranger. "Possibly that's my general classification. To be more specific, however, I'm a ghost."

"Ho! Nonsense!" retorted Parley. "I don't believe in ghosts."

"That may be," said the other, calmly. "I didn't when I was here, a living human being with two legs and a taste for smoke, like you. But I found out afterwards that I was all wrong. When you get to be a ghost, if you have any self-respect you'll believe in 'em. Furthermore, if I wasn't a ghost I couldn't have got in here through two closed doors to speak to you."

"Over the Plum-Pudding"

"That's so," replied Parley. "I didn't think of that. Still, you can't expect me to believe you without some proof. Suppose you let me whack you over the head with this stick? If it goes through you without hurting you, all well and good. If it doesn't, and knocks you out, I sha'n't be any the worse off. What do you say?"

"I'm perfectly willing," said the voice; "only look out for your chair. You might spoil it."

"Afraid, eh?" said Parley.

"For the chair, yes," replied the spirit. "Still it isn't my chair, and if you want to take the risk, I'm willing. You can kick a football through my ribs if you wish. It's all the same to me."

"I'll try the banger," said Parley, dryly. "Then if you are a sneak-thief, as I half suspect, you'll get what you deserve. If you're what you claim to be, all's well for both of us. Shall I?"

"Go ahead," replied the ghost, nonchalantly.

Parley was more surprised than ever, and was beginning to believe that It was a ghost, after all. No sneak-thief would willingly permit himself to be whacked on the head with any such adamantine weapon as that which Parley held in his hand.

"Never mind," said he, relenting. "I won't."

"You *must*, now," said the other. "If you don't, I can't help you at all. I can't be of service to a person who either can't or won't believe in me. If you want to pass your examinations, whack."

"Bah! What idiocy!" cried Parley. "I—"

"Go ahead and whack," persisted the voice. "As hard as you know how, too, if you want to. Pretend you are cornered by a wild beast, and have only one chance to escape, and whack for dear life. I'm ready. My arms are folded, and I'm sitting right here over the embroidered cushion that serves as the seat of your chair."

"I've caught you, there," said Parley. "You aren't sitting there at all. I can see the embroidered cushion."

"Which simply proves what I say," retorted the ghost. "If I were not a ghost, but a material thing like a sneak-thief, you couldn't see through me. Whack away."

47

"Over the Plum-Pudding"

And Parley did so. He raised the banger aloft, and brought it down on the spot where the invisible creature was sitting with all the force at his command.

"There," said the ghost, calmly, from the chair. "Are you satisfied? It didn't do me any damage; though I must say you've knocked the embroidery into smithereens."

It was even as he said. The force with which Parley had brought the heavy stick down had made a great rent in the soft cushion, and he had had his trouble for his pains.

"Well, do you believe in me now?" the ghost demanded, Parley, in his surprise and wrath, having found no words suited to the occasion.

"I suppose I've got to," he replied, ruefully gazing upon the ruined cushion. "That's what I get for being an idiot. I don't know—"

"It's what you get for pretending that you can't believe all that you can't see," put in the ghost, "which is a very grave error for a young man—or an old one, either, for that matter—to make."

PARLEY CONVERSING WITH THE INVISIBLE GHOST

The Flunking of Watkins's Ghost

Parley sat down, and was silent for a moment.

"Well," he said at length, "granting that there are such things as ghosts, and that you are one, what the deuce do you come bothering me for? Just wanted to plague me, I suppose, and get me to smash my furniture."

"Not at all," retorted the ghost. "I didn't ask you to smash your furniture. On the contrary, I warned you that that was what you were going to do. You suggested smashing me, and I told you to go ahead."

Parley couldn't deny it, but he could not quite conceal his resentment.

"Don't you think I'm bothered enough by the prospect of a beautiful flunk at my exams, without your trickling in through the doorway to exasperate me?" he demanded.

"Who has come to exasperate you, Parley?" said the ghost, a trifle irritably. "I haven't. I came to help you, but, by Jingo! I've half a mind to leave you to get out of your troubles the best way you can. Do you know what's the matter with you?

49

"Over the Plum-Pudding"

You are too impetuous. You are the kind of chap who strikes first and thinks afterwards. So far your experiments on me have kept me from telling you who I am and what I've come for. If you don't want help, say so. There are others who do, and I'll be jiggered if I wouldn't rather help them than you, now that I know what a fly-away Jack you are."

The spirit with which the visitor uttered these words made Parley somewhat ashamed of his behavior, and yet no one could really blame him, under the circumstances, for doing what he did.

"I'm sorry," he said, in a moment, "but you must remember, sir, that at Blue Haven there is no chair in manners, and the etiquette of a meeting of this sort is a closed book to me."

"That's all right," returned the ghost, kindly. "I don't blame you, on the whole. The trouble lies just where you say. In college people study geology and physiology and all the other 'ologies, save spectrology. Most college trustees disbelieve in ghosts, just as you do, and the consequence is you only touch upon the relations of man

50

The Flunking of Watkins's Ghost

with the spirit world in your studies of
psychology, and then only in a very incom-
plete fashion. Any gentleman knows how
to behave to another gentleman, but when
he comes into contact with a spook he's all
at sea. If somebody would only write a
ghost-etiquette book, or a 'Spectral Don't,'
people who suffer from what you are pleased
to call hallucinations would have an easier
time of it. If I had been a book-agent, or a
sneak - thief, or a lady selling patent egg-
beaters which no home should be without,
you would have received me with greater
courtesy than you did."

" Still," said Parley, anxious to make
out a good case for himself, " most of 'em
wouldn't walk right into a fellow's room
and scare him to death, you know."

" Nor would I," said the ghost. " You
are still living, Parley, as you wouldn't
have been if I'd scared you to death."

"Specious, but granted," returned Parley.
" And now, Mr. Spook, let's exchange cards."

"I left my card-case at home," laughed
the spirit. "But I'll tell you who I am
and it will suffice. I'm old Billie Watkins,
of the class of ninety-nine."

"Over the Plum-Pudding"

"There is no Watkins in ninety-nine,"said Parley, suspiciously.

"Well, there *was*," retorted the spirit. "I ought to know, because I was old Billie myself. Valedictorian, too."

"What are you talking about?" demanded Parley. "Ninety-nine hasn't graduated yet!"

"Yes, it has," returned the ghost. "Seventeen ninety-nine, I mean."

Parley whistled. "Oh, I see! You're a relic of the last century!"

"That's it; and I can tell you, Parley, we eighteenth-century boys made Blue Haven a very different sort of a place from what you make it," said Billie. "We didn't mind being young, you know. When we had an eight-oared race, we rowed only four men, and each man managed two oars. And there wasn't any fighting over strokes, either; and we'd row anybody that chose to try us. The main principle was to have a race, and the only thing we thought about was getting in first."

"In any old way, I suppose?" sneered Parley.

"You bet!" cried the spirit, with enthusiasm. "We'd have put our eight-oared crew up against twenty Indians in a canoe, if they'd asked us; and when it came to rounders, we could bat balls a mile in those days. A fellow didn't have to make a science out of his fun when I was at Blue Haven."

"And what good did it do you?" cried Parley.

"We held every belt and every mug and every medal in the thirteen States, that's what. We laid out Cambridge at one-old-cat eight times in two months, and as for those New York boys, we beat 'em at marbles on their own campus," returned the ghost.

Parley was beginning to be interested.

"I'd like to see the records of those times," he said.

"Records? Bosh!" said old Billie Watkins. "You don't for a moment believe that every time we played a game of marbles or peg-top, or rowed against a lot of the town boys, we sat down and wrote up a history of it, do you? We were too busy having fun for that. Oh, those days! those days!" the ghost added, with a sigh. "College wasn't filled with politicians and scientific fun-seekers and grandfathers then."

" Grandfathers? More likely you were forefathers," suggested Parley.

" We've become both since," said Watkins. "But we were boys then, and glad of it."

" Aren't we boys now?" queried Parley.

" Yes, you are," replied the ghost. " But you seem to be doing your best to conceal the fact. As soon as a lad gets into college now he puts on all the airs of a man. Walks, talks like a grave man. Eats and drinks like a grave man. Why, I don't believe you ever robbed the president's hen-coop in your life!"

" No," laughed Parley, " never. For two reasons: it's easier to get our chickens cooked at the dining-hall, and Prex hasn't got a hen-coop."

" Exactly. Even our college presidents aren't what they were. Never hooked a ham out of his smoke-house, either, I'll wager, and for the same reason—Prex hasn't a smoke-house. All the smoking he does is in the line of cigars. But all this hasn't got anything to do with what I came here for. I came to help you, and

The Flunking of Watkins's Ghost

I've seen enough of the way things are done in colleges these days to know that in the other respects of which I have spoken you are beyond help. Besides, this help is personal. You are worried about your examinations, aren't you?"

"Well, rather," said Parley. "You see, I've been playing football."

"Precisely," said Watkins. "And you've put so much time into learning to do it scientifically and without using your feet, as we did, that you've let everything else go."

"I suppose so," said Parley, sullenly.

"That's it," said old Billie Watkins. "Now that everything's science, there isn't time for a boy to do more than one thing at a time, and he's got to choose between his degree and seeing his picture in the papers as an athlete. Well, it's not your fault, maybe. It's the times, and I'm going to help you out. I always try to help somebody once a year. It's my Christmas gift to mankind, and this year I've decided to help you out of your fix. Last year I helped Blue Haven win the debating championship as against our traditional rivals. This year I should have tried to get Blue

"Over the Plum-Pudding"

Haven to the fore in the boat-race, but everybody about here was so cocksure of winning it didn't seem to be necessary. I'm sorry now I didn't know it was all men's bluff and not boys' confidence. I might have helped the little men out. Still, that's over, and you are to be the gainer. *I'll pass your examinations for you.*"

"What?" cried Parley, scarcely able to believe his ears.

"I'll pass your examinations for you," repeated the ghost. "It won't be hard. As I told you, I was valedictorian of my class."

"But how?" asked Parley. "You couldn't pass yourself off for me, you know."

"Never said I could," returned Billie Watkins. "Never wanted to. I'd rather be me, floating around in space, than you. What I propose to do is to stand alongside of you, and tell you the answers to your questions."

"But what will the professors say?" demanded Parley.

"How will they know? They won't be able to see me any more than you can," said the ghost. "It's easy as shooting."

56

The Flunking of Watkins's Ghost

"Well, I don't know if it's square," said Parley. "In fact, I do know that it isn't; but if I get through this time I won't get into the same fix again."

"That's just the point," returned the ghost. "You're young, in spite of your trying not to be, and you've got into trouble. I'll help you out once, but after that you'll have to paddle your own steam-yacht. I suppose you scientific watermen wouldn't demean yourselves by paddling a canoe, the way we used to."

"I'm sure I'm very much obliged, Mr. Watkins," said Parley.

"Oh, botheration!" cried the ghost. "*Mister Watkins!* Look here, Parley, we're both Blue Haven boys—somewhat far apart in time, it's true, but none the less Blue-Havenites. Don't 'mister' me. Call me Billie."

"All right, Billie," said Parley. "I'll go you, and after it's all over I'll be as much of a boy as I can."

"That's right," said the ghost of old Billie Watkins, and then he departed. At least I presume he departed, for from that time on to the day of the examinations Parley did not hear his voice again.

"Over the Plum-Pudding"

What happened then can best be explained by the narration of an interview between Parley and the ghost of old Billie Watkins on the night of the concluding examination-day. Sick, tired, and flunked, poor Parley went to his room to bemoan his unhappy fate. In no single branch had he been successful. Apparently his reliance upon the assistance of Watkins's ghost had proved a mistake—as, in fact, it was, although poor old Watkins was, as it turned out, no more to blame than if he had never volunteered his services.

Flinging himself down in despair, Parley gave way to his feelings.

"That's what I get for being an ass and believing in ghosts. I might have known it was all a dream," he groaned.

"It wasn't," said the unmistakable voice of Watkins, from the chair, which had been repaired.

Parley jumped as if stung.

"You're a gay old valedictorian, you are!" he cried, glowering at the chair. "Next time you have a Christmas gift for mankind, take it and burn it, will you? A pretty fix you've got me into."

The Flunking of Watkins's Ghost

"I'm sorry, Parley," began the ghost. "I—"

"Sorry be hanged!" cried Parley. "If you hadn't made me believe in you, I might have crammed up on my Greek and Latin anyhow. As it is, it's a Waterloo all around."

"If you won't listen—" the ghost began again.

"I've listened enough!" roared Parley, thoroughly enraged. "And if there was any way in which I could get at you, I'd make you smart for your low-down trick!"

"To think," moaned the ghost, "that I should see the day when old Billie Watkins was accused of a low-down trick—and I tried to help him, too."

"Tried to help me?" sneered Parley. "How the deuce do you make that out? You didn't come within a mile of me, and I've not only flunked, but I've lost a half-dozen bets on my ability to pass, just because I believed in you."

"I *was* within a mile of you," retorted the ghost, indignantly. "I was **right** square in front of you."

"Then why the dickens didn't you an-

59

"Over the Plum-Pudding"

swer the questions? I read 'em out so loud
that old Professor Wiggins sat on me for
it."

"I know you did, Parley," said the ghost,
meekly. "And I'd have answered 'em if
I could. But I couldn't."

"Couldn't?" cried Parley.

"Regularly just couldn't," said the ghost.

'A valedictorian couldn't answer a
question on a Freshman's paper?" cried
Parley, scornfully.

"No," said the ghost.

"Fine memory you must have! Do you
know what a-b, ab, spells?" sneered Parley.

"I do, of course," retorted the ghost,
angrily. "A-b, ab, spells nothing. But
that doesn't prove anything I remember
all I ever learned at Blue Haven, but I've
made a discovery. Parley, which lets me
out. You ought to have told me, but, my
dear fellow, college begins now just about
where it used to leave off."

"What?" queried Parley, doubtfully.
"What do you mean?"

"Why, it's plain enough, Jack! Can't
you see?" said Watkins. "What would

make a valedictorian in my day won't help
a Freshman through his first year now.
Times have changed."

"Oh, that's it—eh?" said Parley, somewhat mollified. "It isn't only the fellows
that have changed and their sports, but
the curriculum—eh? That it?"

"Precisely," rejoined old Billie, with a
sigh of relief that Parley should understand him. "I'm beginning to understand, my boy, why you fellows have to be
little men and not boys. No average boy
could pass any such stiff paper as that, and
I found myself as ignorant as you are."

"Thanks," said Parley, with a short
laugh. "I think you ought to have found
it out before leading me into accepting your
Christmas gift, though."

"It was you who should have found out
and told me," retorted the ghost. "All I
can say is that in my day I'd have got you
through with flying colors."

"Well, I'm much obliged," said Parley.
"I'll get out of it somehow, but it means
hard work; only, Mr. Spook, don't be so
free with your Christmas gifts another
time."

"Over the Plum-Pudding"

"I won't, Jack," said the spirit—"that is, I won't if you'll forgive me and stop calling me mister. Call me Billie again, and show you've forgiven me."

"All right, Billie, my boy," said Parley. "We'll call it square."

And the unhappy ghost wandered off into the night, leaving Parley to fight his battles alone. Whether he has turned up again or not, I am not aware, but, from my observation of Jack Parley's ways ever since, I think he really did learn something from his contact with Billie Watkins's ghost. He has been a good deal of a boy ever since. As for Watkins, I hope that the genial old soul off in space somewhere has also learned something from Jack. If the old chaps and the youngsters can only get together and appreciate one another's good points, and how each has had to labor towards the same end under possibly different conditions, there will be a greater harmony and sympathy between them, and they will discover that, in spite of differing times and differing customs, 'way down at bottom they are the same old wild animals, after all. There is no more delightful spectacle anywhere than that to be seen at a college gathering, where the patriarchs of the fifties and the Freshmen of the present join hand-in-hand and lark it together, and it is this spirit that makes for the glory of Alma Mater everywhere.

So, after all, perhaps the meeting of Jack Parley and old Billie Watkins's ghost had its value. For my part, I can only hope that it had, and leave them both with my blessing.

An Unmailed Letter

An Unmailed Letter

I CALLED the other night at the home of my friend Jack Chetwood, and found him, as usual, engaged in writing. Chetwood's name is sufficiently well known to all who read books and periodicals these days to spare me the necessity of adverting to his work, or of attempting to describe his personality. It is said that Chetwood writes too much. Indeed, I am one of those who have said so, and I have told *him* so. His response has always been that I—and others who have ventured to remonstrate —did not understand. He had to keep at it, he said. Couldn't help himself. Didn't write for fun, but because he had to. Always did his best, anyhow, and what more can be asked of any man? Surely a de-

67

fence of this nature takes the wind out of
a critic's sails.

"Busy, Jack?" said I, as I en'ered his
sanctum.

"Yes," said he. "Very."

"Very well," said I. "Don't let me disturb you. I only happened in, anyhow.
Nothing in particular to say; but, Jacky,
why don't you quit for a little? You're
worn and pale and thin. What's the use
of breaking down? Don't pose with me.
You don't have to write all the time."

He smiled wanly at me.

"I—I'm only writing a letter this time,"
he said.

"Oh, in that case—' I began.

"You can't guess whom to?" he interrupted.

"Me," said I.

"No," he retorted. "Me."

"I don't understand," said I, somewhat
perplexed.

"Myself," laughed Chetwood.

"You are writing a letter to—to—"

"Myself," said he. "Truly so. Odd,
isn't it? Wait a few minutes, old man,
and I'll read it to you. Light a cigar

and sit down just a minute and I'll be through."

I lit one of Chetwood's cigars. They are excellent. I have heard one expert pronounce them "bully." They are, and of course while I smoked I was happy.

At the end of a half-hour's waiting, the silence broken only by the scratching of Chetwood's pen and by my own puffings upon the weed, he wheeled about in his chair.

"Well, that's finished," he said, and he glanced affectionately and, I thought, wistfully about his charming workshop.

"Good," said I. "You promised to read it to me."

"All right," said he. "Here goes."

And he kept his word. I reproduce the letter from memory. Like all copy-mongers, he began it with a title double underscored, and I reproduce it as I heard it:

"LETTER TO MYSELF

"ON CHRISTMAS GIVING: A HINT

"MY DEAR JOHN,—As the Christmas holidays approach it has seemed to me to be somewhat in the line of my duty to write to you not only to wish you

"Over the Plum-Pudding"

all the good things of the season, but to give you a little fatherly advice which may stand you in good stead when the first of January comes about. I have observed you and your ways with some particularity for some time; in fact, since that very happy day, nearly twenty years ago, when you entered upon the duties of citizenship, with twenty-one years and a birthday gift of $500 from your father to your credit. The twenty-one years had come easily and had gone easily. All you had had to do to acquire and to retain them was to breathe and to keep your feet dry. The $500, which represented so much toil on your father's part, came to you quite as easily. You saw the check, and you realized the possibilities of the sum for which it called, but I do not think you ever realized the effort that produced that $500. I judge from the way you let it filter through your fingers that you thought your generous father picked the money up from a pile of gold lying somewhere in the back yard of his home. I do not know if you recall what it went for, but I do. Some of it went for a half-dozen sporting pictures of some rarity that you had long wished to hang on the walls of your den. More of it went for rare first editions of books whose possession you had envied others for no little time. A portion of it was spent on sundry trinkets which should adorn your person. such as studs, scarf-pins, a snake ring, with ruby eyes — a disgusting-looking thing, by the way—to encircle your little finger. There were also certain small things in the line of bronzes, silver writing implements, a jug or two of some value that you had cast your eyes upon, and which you were

70

An Unmailed Letter

quick to acquire. Do you remember, my dear Jack, how delighted you were with all that you were able to buy with that $500, until the bills came in and you found that the consciousness of a $500 backing had led you into an expenditure of a trifle over $900? You were painfully surprised that day, Jacky, my boy, but, as I have watched you since you let it go at that, you never learned anything from those bills. Indeed, what you call your cheerful philosophy, which led you to console yourself then with the thought that the stuff you had bought on credit if sold at auction would bring in enough to pay the deficit, has clung to you ever since, and has served you ill—very ill—unless I am wholly mistaken. You would strike any other man than myself were he to venture to call you a second Mr. Micawber, but Johnnie, dear, that is what you are —and you are even worse than that, John. Let me assure you of the fact. *You are something worse.* You are a modern Dick Turpin! Don't be angry at my saying so. Merely understand that I am telling you the truth, and for your own good, and I'll explain the analogy. I cannot call a man a modern Dick Turpin without explaining why I do so.

" Turpin was a highwayman, as you know. He mounted his horse and went out upon the highway, and whatever he wanted he took. He had no greater powers of resistance in the face of temptation than others had in the face of him. You, John, are much the same, even if you do not realize the fact. You mount the steed called Credit, and you go out upon the highways, and whatever you see that you happen to want you take—don't you, Jack? It is true that,

71

sooner or later, you pay, but so did Turpin. Turpin paid with his life. You will pay with yours, and that is why I write you, for the constant anxiety to meet the obligations of your thefts—for that is what they are, John; we cannot blink the fact—this constant anxiety, I say, is sapping your strength, undermining your constitution, destroying slowly but surely your nerves, and sooner or later you will succumb to the strain. Is it worth the price, my boy?

"I can imagine you asking what all this has to do with Christmas and the season of Peace on Earth and Good Will to Man. You think I am merely cavilling, but I am not. It has this to do with it: It involves my Christmas present to you, which is important to me and I trust will be so to you. I am not going to give you a gold watch, or a complete edition of Thackeray, or a set of golf clubs this year, and, being a man, I cannot knit you a worsted vest as your sister might —or as some other fellow's sister might. All I can afford to give you this year is a hint, and I shall not wait until Christmas morn to hand it over to you, because it would then lack value. I send it to you now, when you need it most, and, if you accept it, when the Christmas chimes begin to sound their music on the frosty air you will thank me for it perhaps more than you do now.

"Don't be a highwayman this year, John. Never mind what Solomon said; think of what I say. Solomon was a wise man, but he lived in a bygone age. Take thought of the morrow, my boy. Don't consider the lilies of the field, but come down to real business. Don't mount your prancing horse Credit and

72

An Unmailed Letter

hold up some poor jeweller for a silver water-pitcher for your brother George when you know that on January 1st the jeweller will probably ask you for a *quid pro quo*, and for which *quid* you will be compelled to compel him to wait until April or May. And remember that, if your dear wife could have her choice, she would infinitely prefer your peace of mind to the sables which you propose to give her at Christmas, bought on a credit which, however pleasing to-day, is sure to become a very pressing annoyance to-morrow.

" Then, my dear man, there are your children. What a joy they are! What a source of affectionate pride; what a source of satisfaction, and how they trust you, Jack. You remember the trust you placed in your father. You have never slept since you had to do for yourself as you slept when he did for you. You didn't know a care then; you had no worries in those old days; you knew your home was yours and that every reasonable thing you could wish for he would give you to the full extent of his means. That confidence was not misplaced, and all that you have to-day you'd willingly give up for that sweet peace of mind that was yours while he was with you. God bless him and his memory. Do you realize, Jack, that you occupy that same relation to your children? They believe in you as you believed in him. And are you meeting your responsibilities as he met his? Think it over. Of course, for instance, Tommie wants a complete railway system, with tracks and signals and switches and nickel-plated rolling stock, and all that—but can you afford to give it to him? And

"Over the Plum-Pudding"

Pollie—dear little Pollie—what right-minded little Pollie does not want a doll; a great yellow-haired, blue-eyed, pink-cheeked doll, with automatic insides and an expensive trousseau? But can you really afford to give it to her? Do you remember when you were a baby how you wanted the moon, and yelled for it lustily? And do you remember how you didn't get it, and how you sobbed yourself to sleep, and how, in spite of it all, you waked up the next morning all smiles and sunshine, with no recollection of ever having wanted the moon? And do you realize that if your daddy *could* have given it to you he *would* have done so? Do you recollect how. ever since that happy time, you have wanted the earth, and how you haven't got it, and how fortunate you are, and how happy you are without it? So it is, and so it will be with your children. These things do not change. My beloved boy, a serene, unworried father, next to a serene and happy mother, is God's most gracious gift to childhood, at Christmas or at any other time. If January finds you petulant and nervous over a bill you cannot pay for Tommie's Christmas railway and for Pollie's Yuletide doll, then has the 25th of December brought woe instead of joy into your home; strife instead of peace, and good will to man is not to be found there. In January the pure, sweet, simple little minds will wonder at you, Jack. The little hearts will love you just the same, but the little minds will wonder at your irritability, and they will still hold to that beautiful trust. And you? Well, you'll toss about at night, sleepless and worried, and if you are of the right sort, as I hope and believe you are, you will ask yourself

An Unmailed Letter

if you are worthy of the confidence the little ones place in you. Your mistaken notions of generosity may have imperilled your household. Given health and strength and ideas, you may be able to keep on and make all right, but who knows at what moment you will have to give up the fight? Why should you invite care and worry? Why not come down to the serious facts and insure the happiness of all who depend upon you by following out a sane and sensible plan of living and of giving? My dear boy, don't you know you are doing wrong in being unjustifiably ostentatious in your giving? I have likened you to Turpin. You will laugh this off. You aren't a thief—at least you cannot believe that you are one; but there is something worse even than being a thief, and I fear you are verging upon it.

"Frankly, Jack, I am afraid you are a snob. Yes, sir, a plain snob; and if snobbery is not worse than thievery, I know nothing of life. I'd rather be a straight-out, sincere, honest, unpretending thief than a snob, my dear boy. Wouldn't you? Let us look into this. The thief is the creature of circumstances. He is what he is because his environment and his moral sense, plus his necessities, require that he shall do what he does. But the snob—what compelling circumstances make a snob of a man? Why should he make a pretence of being what he is not? Why should he give things he cannot afford to give unless it be that he desires to make an impression that he has no right to? The thief banks on nothing. The snob takes advantage of his supposed respectability. Bless us, Jacky, aren't *we* worse than they are?

"Over the Plum-Pudding"

" Read your Thackeray, old chap. See what he said about snobs. *He* never inveighed against the submerged soul that never had a chance. He never, with all his imputed cynicism, made a slimy thing of those who fell, as Dickens did. He struck high. He exploited the vices of those who might do him real harm. He took the high man, not the low man, for his target, and he struck home when he struck at snobbery. And he struck a blow for purer, sweeter living, and men may call him cynic for all time, but I shall never cease to call him brave and true for what he did for you and for me, as well as for all other men.

" Put yourself in the crucible, Jack. Find out what you are and what you may be, and don't try to make yourself appear to be generous when you are simply financially reckless. Don't rob your creditors in the vain hope that you are living up to the spirit of the hour, and don't rob yourself. You are not living up to that spirit. You are degrading it. God knows I love you more than I love any living thing except my wife and children, but let me tell you this: the man who gives more than he has a right to give is a thief in the eyes of conscience, and, worse than that, he is a snob, and a mean one at that. Adapt your giving to your circumstances. Do what you can to make others happy, but at this season do not, I beg of you, try to do what you can't in an effort to appear for what you are not.

" The happiness of your children, of your wife, of yourself, is involved, and when that happiness is attacked or weakened, then is the whole spirit of Christmas season set aside, and the selfishness of the posing impostor put in its place. Always your affectionate self,

"JOHN HENRY CHETWOOD."

When Chetwood had finished I puffed away fiercely upon my cigar.

"Good letter, Jack," said I.

"Yes," said he, tearing it up.

"Don't do that," I cried, trying to restrain him.

He smiled again and sighed. "It's —gone," said he. "Gone. Forever. I shall never write it again."

"You should have sent it to—to yourself," said I. "I have thought sometimes that such a letter should be written to you."

"Possibly," said he. "But—it's gone." And he tossed it into the waste-basket.

"It's a pity," said I. "You—you might have sold that."

"I know I might," said he. "But if it had ever appeared in print I should have been immortally mad. It's a libel on myself. Truth—is libellous, you know."

"It might have been rejected," I said, sarcastically.

"That would have made me madder yet," said Chetwood.

"Over the Plum-Pudding"

"Still—you realize the—ah—situation, Jack," I put in.

"Well," said he, with a laugh, "Christmas is coming, and when the fever is on—I—well, I catch it. I want to give, give, give, and give I shall."

"But you are imperilling—" I cried.

"I know, I know," he interrupted, gently. "God knows I know, but it is the fever of the hour. You can't stave off an epidemic. It's not my fault; it's the fault of the times."

"Nonsense," I retorted. "Can't you stand up against the times?"

"I can," said he, complacently lighting a cigar. "But I sha'n't. We'll all go to ruin together. The man who tries to stand up against the spirit of the times is an ass. I lack the requisite number of legs for that."

"Well," I put in, "I wish you a merry Christmas—"

"I shall have it," said he, cheerily. "The children—"

"And the New Year?" I interrupted.

"It isn't here yet," said Chetwood. "And I never cross a bridge until I come to it. Take another cigar."

An Unmailed Letter

Nevertheless, I went from Chetwood that night rather happier than I ought to have been, perhaps. His letter, even though he did not choose to mail it to himself, showed that he was thinking—thinking about it; and I was glad.

What if all men were to consider the questions that Chetwood raised?

Might not the meaning of Christmas, with all its joy and all its beauty, and all its inspiration-giving qualities, once more be made clear to man? I for one believe it would, and I venture to hope that the old-time simplicity of the observance of the day may again be restored unto us.

"God bless us all!" said Tiny Tim.

When the simpler, happier Christmas time, which is a joy, and not a burden, comes back to us, then will Tiny Tim's prayer have been answered.

The Amalgamated Brotherhood
of Spooks

The Amalgamated Brotherhood
of Spooks

A LETTER TO THE EDITOR

I T is with very deep regret that I
find myself unable to keep the
promise made to you last spring
to provide you with a suitable
ghost story for your Christmas number.
I have made several efforts to prepare such
a tale as it seemed to me you would require,
but, one and all, these have proved unavail-
ing. By a singular and annoying combination of circumstances in which only my
unfortunate habit of meeting trouble in a
spirit of badinage has involved me, I cannot
secure the models which I invariably need
for the realistic presentation of my stories,
and I decline at this present, as I have
hitherto consistently declined, to draw upon
my imagination for the ingredients necessary, even though tempted by the exigencies

of a contract sealed, signed, and delivered. It is far from my wish to be known to you as one who makes promises only to break them, but there are times in a man's life when he must consider seriously which is the lesser evil, to deceive the individual or to deceive the world, the latter being a mass of individuals, and, consequently, as much more worthy of respect as the whole is greater than a part. Could I bring myself to be false to my principles as a scribe, and draw upon my fancy for my facts, and, through a prostitution of my art, so sickly o'er my plot with the pale cast of realism as to hoodwink my readers into believing what I know to be false, the task were easy. Given a more or less active and unrestrained imagination, pen, ink, paper, and the will to do so, to construct out of these a ghost story which might have been, but as a matter of fact was not, presents no difficulties whatsoever; but I unfortunately have a conscience which, awkward as it is to me at times, I intend to keep clear and unspotted. The consciousness of having lied would forever rest as a blot upon my escutcheon. I cannot manufacture out of whole cloth a narrative such as you desire and be true to myself, and this I intend to be, even if by so doing I must seem false to you. I think, however, that, as one of my friends and most important consumer, you are entitled to a complete explanation. of my failure to do as I have told you I would. To most others I should send merely a curt note evidencing, not pleading, a pressure of other work as the cause of my not coming to time. To you it is owed that I should enter somewhat into the details of the unfortunate business.

You doubtless remember that last summer, with our mutual friend Peters, I travelled abroad seeking health and, incidentally, ideas. I had discovered that imported ideas were on the whole rather more popular in America than those which might be said to be indigenous to the soil. The reading public had, for the time being at least, given itself over to moats and châteaux and bloodshed and the curious dialects of the lower orders of British society. Sherlock Holmes had superseded Old Sleuth in the affections of my countrymen who read books. Even those honest little critics the

"Over the Plum-Pudding"

boys and girls were finding more to delight them in the doings of Richard Cœur de Lion and Alice in Wonderland than in the more remarkable and intensely American adventures of Ragged Dick or Mickie the Motorboy. John Storm was at that moment hanging over the world like the sword of Damocles, and Rudolf Rassendyll had completely overshadowed such essentially American heroes as Uncle Tom and Rollo. I found, to my chagrin, that the poetry of Tennyson was more widely read even than my own, even though Tennyson was dead and I was not. And in the universities whole terms were devoted to the compulsory study of dramatists like Shakespeare and Molière, while home talent, as represented by Mr. Hoyt or the facile productions of Messrs. Weber & Fields, was relegated to the limbo of electives which the students might take up or not, as they chose, and then only in the hours which they were expected to devote to recreation. All of which seemed to indicate that while there was of course no royal road to literary fame, there was with equal certainty no republican path thereto, and that real inspiration was to be derived rather under the effete monarchies of Europe than at home. To Peters the same idea had occurred, but in his case in relation to art rather than to literature. The patrons of art in America had a marked preference for the works of Meissonier, Corot, Gérôme, Millet—anybody, so long as he was a foreigner, Peters said. The wealthy would pay ten, twenty, a hundred thousand dollars for a Rousseau or a Rosa Bonheur rather than exchange a paltry one hundred dollars for a canvas by Peters, though, as far as Peters was concerned, his canvas was just as well woven, his pigments as carefully mixed, and his application of the one to the other as technically correct as was anything from the foreign brushes.

"You can't take in the full import of a Turner unless you stand a way away from it," said he, "and if you'll only stand far enough away from mine you couldn't tell it from a Meissonier."

And when I jocularly responded to this that I thought a mile was the proper distance, he was offended. We quarrelled, but made up after a while, and in the making up decided upon a little venture into

"Over the Plum-Pudding"

foreign fields together, not only to recuperate, but to see if so be we could discover just where the workers on the other side got that quality which placed them in popular esteem so far ahead of ourselves.

What we discovered along this especial line must form the burden of another story. The main cause of our foreign trip, these discoveries, are but incidental to the theme I have in hand. Our conclusions were important, but they have no place here, and what they were you will have to wait until my work on *Abroad versus Home* is completed to learn. But what is important to this explanation is the fact that while going through the long passage leading from the Pitti Palace to the Uffizi Gallery at Florence we—or rather I—encountered one of those phantoms which have been among the chief joys and troubles of my life. Peters was too much taken up with his Baedeker to see either ghosts or pictures. Indeed, it used to irritate me that Peters saw so little, but he would do as most American tourists do, and spend all of his time looking for some especial thing he thought he ought to see, and generally missing not only

"I THOUGHT A MILE WAS THE PROPER DISTANCE"

it, but thousands of minor things quite as well worthy of his attention. I don't believe he would have seen the ghost, however, under any circumstances. It requires a specially cultivated eye or digestion, one or the other, to enable one to see ghosts, and Peters's eye is blind to the invisible and his digestion is good.

Why, under the canopy, the vulgar little spectre was haunting a picture-gallery I never knew, unless it was to embarrass the Americans who passed to and fro, for he claimed to be an American spook. I knew he was not a living thing the minute I laid eyes through him. He loomed up before me while I was engaged in chuckling over a particularly bad canvas by somebody whose name I have forgotten, but which was something like Beppo di Contarini. It represented the scene of a grand fête at Venice back in the fifteenth century, and while preserved by the art-lovers of Florence as something worthy, would, I firmly believe, have failed of acceptance even by the catholic taste of the editor of an American Sunday newspaper comic supplement. The thing was crude in its drawing, impossible

in its coloring, and absolutely devoid of
action.   Every gondola on the canal looked
as if it were stuck in the mud, and as for
the water of the Grand Canal itself, it had
all the liquid glory under this artist's touch
of calf's-foot jelly, and it amused me intensely to think that these patrons of art,
in the most artistic city in the world, should
have deemed it worth keeping.   However,
whatever the merit of the painting, I was
annoyed in the midst of my contemplation
of it to have thrust into the line of vision a
shape—I cannot call it a body because there
was no body to it.   There were the linea-
ments of a living person, and a very vulgar
living person at that, but the thing was
translucent, and as it stepped in between
me and the wonderful specimen of Beppo di
Somethingorother's art I felt as if a sudden
haze had swept over my eyes, blurring the
picture until it reminded me of a cheap
kind of decalcomania that in my boyhood
days had satisfied my yearnings after the
truly beautiful.

I made several ineffectual passes with my
hands to brush the thing away.   I had
discovered   that   with   certain   classes   of

ghosts one could be rid of them, just as one may dissipate a cloud of smoke, by swirling one's outstretched paw around in it, and I hoped that I might in this way rid myself of the nuisance now before me. But I was mistaken. He swirled, but failed to dissipate.

"Hum!" said I, straightening up, and addressing the thing with some degree of irritation. "You may know a great deal about art, my friend, but you seem not to have studied manners. Get out of my way."

"Pah!" he ejaculated, turning a particularly nasty pair of green eyes on me. "Who the deuce are you, that you should give me orders?"

"Well," said I, "if I were impulsive of speech and seldom grammatical, I might reply by saying Me, but as a purist, let me tell you, sir, that I'm I, and if you seek to know further and more intimately, I will add that who I am is none of your infernal business."

"Humph!" he said, shrugging his shoulders. "Grammatical or otherwise, you're a coward! You don't dare say who you are, because you are afraid of me. You know I am a spectre, and, like all commonplace people, you are afraid of ghosts."

A hot retort was on my lips, and I was about to tell him my name and address, when it occurred to me that by doing so I might lay myself open to a kind of persecution from which I have suffered from time to time, ghosts are sometimes so hard to lay, so I accomplished what I at the moment thought was my purpose by a bluff.

"Oh, as for that," said I, "my name is So and So, and I live at Number This, That Street, Chicago, Illinois."

Both the name and the address were of course fictitious.

"Very well," said he, calmly, making a note of the address. "My name is Jones. I am the president of the Amalgamated Brotherhood of Spooks, enjoying a well-earned rest from his labors on his savings from his salary as a walking delegate. You shall hear from me on your return to Chicago through the local chapter, the United Apparitions of Illinois."

"All right," said I, with equal calmness. "If the Illinois spooks are as Illinoisome as you are, I will summon the board of health and have them laid without more ado."

Upon this we parted. That is to say, I walked on to the Uffizi, and he vanished, in something of a rage, it seemed to me.

I thought no more of the matter until a week ago, when, in accordance with an agreement with the principal thereof, I left New York to go to Chicago, to give a talk before a certain young ladies' boarding-school, on the subject of "Muscular Romanticism." This was a lecture I had prepared on a literary topic concerning which I had thought much. I had observed that a great deal of the popularity of certain authors had come from the admiration of young girls—mostly those at boarding-school, and therefore deprived of real manly company—for a kind of literature which, seeming to be manly, did not yet appeal very strongly to men. In certain aspects it seemed strong. It presented heroes who were truly heroic, and who always did the right thing in the right manner. Writers who had more ink than blood to shed, and a greater knowledge of etiquette than of

"Over the Plum-Pudding"

human nature, were making their way into temporary fame by compelling chaps to do things they could not do. I rather like to read of these fellows myself. I am no exception to the rule which makes human beings admire, and very strongly, too, the fellow who poses successfully. Indeed, I admire a *poseur* who can carry his pose through without disaster to himself, because he has nothing to back him up, and, wanting this, if by his assurance he can make himself a considerable personage he falls short of genius only by lacking it. But this is apart from the story. Whatever the general line of thought in the lecture, I was, as I have said, on my way to Chicago to deliver it before a young ladies' boarding-school. I should have been happy over the prospect, for I have many warm friends in Chicago, there was a moderately large fee ahead, and there is always a charm, as well, in the mere act of standing on a dais before some two or three hundred young girls and having their undivided attention for a brief hour. Yet, despite all this, I was dreadfully depressed. Why, I could not at first surmise. It seemed to me, however,

"HE VANISHED IN SOMETHING OF A RAGE"

as though some horrid disaster were impending. I experienced all the sensations which make four o'clock in the morning so dreaded an hour to those who suffer from insomnia. My heart would race ahead, thumping like the screw of an ocean greyhound, and then slow down until it seemingly ceased to beat altogether; my hands were alternately dry and hot, and clammy and cold; and then like a flash I knew why, and what it was I feared. It suddenly dawned upon my mind that, by some frightfully unhappy coincidence, the address of Miss Brockton's Academy for Young Ladies, whither I was bound, was precisely the same as that I had given the vulgar little spook at Florence as my own. I had entirely forgotten the incident; and then, as I drew near to the spot whereon I was to have been made to suffer through the machinations of the local chapter of the Amalgamated Brotherhood of Spooks, my soul was filled with dread. Had Grand - Master - Spook Jones's threat been merely idle? Had he, even as I had done, dismissed the whole affair as unworthy of any further care, or would he keep his word?—indeed, had he kept his

word, and, through his followers in the
Amalgamated Brotherhood, made himself
obnoxious to the residents of Number This,
That Street?

My nervous dread redoubled as I neared
Chicago, and it was as much as I could do,
when the train reached Kalamazoo, to keep
from turning back. And the event showed
that I suffered with only too much reason,
for, on my arrival at the home of the in-
stitution, I found it closed. The door was
locked, the shades pulled down, the building the perfect picture of gloom. Miss
Brockton, I was informed, was in a lunatic-
asylum, and two hundred and eighty-three
young girls, ranging from fourteen to
twenty years of age, had been returned to
their parents, the hair of every mother's
daughter of them blanched white as the
driven snow. No one knew, my informant
said, exactly what had occurred at the
academy, but the fact that was plain to all
was that, some two weeks previous to my
coming, the school had retired at the usual
hour one night, in the very zenith of a happy
prosperity, and gathered at breakfast the
next morning to find itself wrecked, and

bearing the outward semblance of a home for indigent old ladies. No one, from Miss Brockton herself to the youngest pupil, could give a coherent account of what had turned them all gray in a single night, and brought the furrows of age to cheeks both old and young, nor could any inducement be held out to any of the pupils to pass another night within those walls. They one and all fled madly back to their homes, and Miss Brockton's attempted explanation was so incredible that, protesting her sanity, she was nevertheless placed under restraint, pending a full investigation of the incident. She had, I was informed, asserted that some sixty ghosts of most terrible aspect had paraded through the house between the hours of midnight and 2 A.M., howling and shrieking and threatening the occupants in a most terrifying fashion. At their head marched a spectre brass-band of twenty-four pieces, grinding out with horrid contortions and grimaces the most awful discords imaginable—discords, indeed, Miss Brockton had said, alongside of which those of the most grossly material German street band in creation became melodies of

soothing sweetness. The spectre rabble
to the rear bore transparencies, upon which
were painted such legends as, "Hail to
Jones, our beloved Chief!" "Strike One,
Strike All!" and, "Down with Hawkins,
the Grinder of Ghosts!" This last caused
my heart to sink still lower, for Hawkins
was the name I had given the vision at
Florence, and I now understood all. It was
only too manifest that I was the cause of the
undoing of these innocents.

My lie to Jones had brought this disaster upon the Brockton Academy. The
dreadfulness of it appalled me, and I
turned away, sick at heart, only to find
myself face to face with the horrid Jones,
grinning like the cad he had proved himself.

"Well, you have done it," I cried, trem-
bling with rage. "I hope you are proud
of yourself, venting your spite on an innocent woman and two hundred and eighty-
three defenceless girls."

He laughed.

"It was a pretty successful haunt," he
said; "and possibly, now that Mrs. Hawkins and your daughters—"

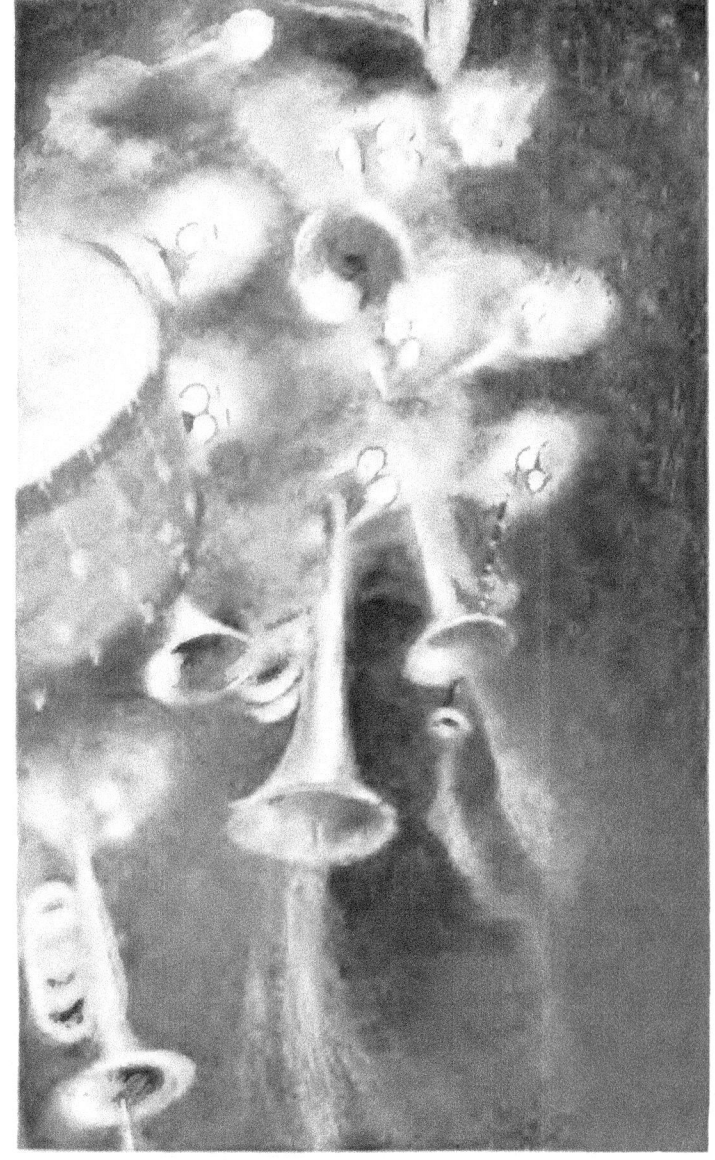

THE SPECTRE BRASS-BAND

"Who?" I cried. "Mrs. What, and my which?"

"Your wife and children," he replied. "Now that the local chapter has attended to them, maybe you'll apologize to me for your boorish behavior at Florence."

"Those people were nothing to me," said I. "That was a boarding-school you have driven crazy. I was merely coming here to lecture—"

I immediately perceived my mistake. He could now easily discover my identity.

"Oho!" said he, with a broad, grim smile. "Then you lied to me at Florence, and you are not Hawkins, but the man they call the spook Boswell among us?"

"Yes, I am not Hawkins, and I am the other," I retorted. "Make the most of it."

"I thought that was rather a large family of girls for one man to have," rejoined Jones. "But see here—are you going to apologize or not?"

"I am not," I cried. "Never in this world nor in the next, you miserable handful of miasma!"

"Then, sir," said he, firmly, "I shall order a general strike for the Amalgamated

Brotherhood of Spooks, and the strike will
be on until you do apologize. Hereafter
you will have to derive your inspiration
from a contemplation of unskilled spooks,
and, if I understand matters, you will find
some difficulty in raising even these, for
there is not one that I know of who doesn't
belong to the union."

With that he vanished, and I sadly made
my way back to my home. Once at my
desk again, I turned my attention to the
work I had promised you, and, to my chagrin,
discovered that while I had in mind all the
ingredients of a successful Christmas story,
I could not write it, because Grand-Master-
Spirit Jones had kept his word. One and
all, my selected group of spooks went out on
strike. They absolutely refused to pose
unless I apologized to Jones, and by no per-
suasions, threats, or cajoling have I been
able since to make them rise up before me,
that I might present them to my readers
with that degree of fidelity which I deem
essential. My home, which was once a sort
of spirit club, is now bare of even a semblance of a ghost worth writing up, and,
conjure as I may, I cannot bring them

"THE THING FELL OVER, LIMP"

back. The strike is on, and I am its victim. But one miserable little specimen have I discovered since my interview with Jones, and so unskilled is he in the science of spooking that I give you my word he could not make a baby shiver on a dark night with the temperature twenty below zero and the wind howling like a madman without; and as for making hair stand on end, I tried him on a bit of hirsute from the tail of the timidest fawn in the Central Park zoo, and the thing fell over as limp as a strand from the silken locks of the Lorelei.

That, my dear sir, is why I cannot give you the story I have promised. I hope you will understand that the fault is not my own, but is the result of the evil tendency of the times, when the protective principle has reached the ultimate of tyrannous absurdity.

While Jones is at the head of the Amalgamated Brotherhood my case is hopeless, for I shall never apologize, unless he promises to restore to poor Mrs. Brockton and her two hundred and eighty-three pupils their former youthful gayety and prosperity, which, I understand upon inquiry, he is unable to do, since the needed patent reversible spook, who will restore blanched hair to its natural color and return the bloom of youth to furrowed cheeks, has not yet been invented; and I, the only person in the world who might have invented it, am powerless, for while the boycott hangs over my head, as you will see for yourself, I am bereft of the raw material for the conducting of the necessary experiments.

A Glance Ahead

A Glance Ahead

BEING A CHRISTMAS TALE OF A.D. 3568

UST how it came about, or how he came to get so far ahead, Dawson never knew, but the details are, after all, unimportant. It is what happened, and not how it happened, that concerns us. Suffice it to say that as he waked up that Christmas morning, Dawson became conscious of a great change in himself. He had gone to bed the night before worn in body and weary in spirit. Things had not gone particularly well with him through the year. Business had been unwontedly dull, and his efforts to augment his income by an occasional operation on the Street had brought about precisely the reverse of that for which he had hoped. This morning, however, all seemed right again. His troubles had in some way become mere memories of a remote past. So far from feeling bodily fatigue, which had been a pressingly insistent sensation of his waking moments of late, he experienced a startling sense of absolute freedom from all physical limitation whatsoever. The room in which he slept seemed also to have changed. The pictures on the walls were not only not the same pictures that had been there when he had gone to bed the night before, but appeared, even as he watched them, to change in color and in composition, to represent real action rather than a mere semblance thereof.

"Humph!" he muttered, as a lithograph copy of "The Angelus" before him went through a process of enlivenment wherein the bell actually did ring, the peasants bowing their heads as in duty bound, and then resuming their work again. "I feel like a bird, but I must be a trifle woozy. I never saw pictures behave that way before." Then he tried to stretch himself, and observed, with a feeling of mingled astonishment and alarm, that he had nothing to stretch with. He had no legs, no arms—no body at all. He was about to indulge in an ejaculation of dismay, but there was no time for it, for, even as he began, a terrifying sound, as of rushing horses, over his bed attracted his attention. Investigation showed that this was caused by an engraving of Gérôme's "Chariot Race," which hung on the wall above his pillow—an engraving which held the same peculiar attributes that had astonished him in the marvellous lithograph of "The Angelus" opposite. The thing itself was actually happening up there. The horses and chariots would appear in the perspective rushing madly along the course, and then, reaching the limits of the frame, would disappear, apparently into thin air, amid the shoutings and clamorings of the pictured populace. Three times it looked as if a mass of horseflesh, chariots, charioteers, and dust would be precipitated upon the bed, and if Dawson could have found his head there is no doubt whatever that he would have ducked it.

"I must get out of this," he cried. "But," he added, as his mind reverted to his disembodied condition, "how the deuce can I? What 'll I get out with?"

"Over the Plum-Pudding"

The answer was instant. By the mere
exercise of the impulse to be elsewhere the
wish was gratified, and Dawson found
himself opposite the bureau which stood
at the far end of the room.

"Wonder how I look without a body?"
he thought, as he ranged his faculties before the glass. But the mirror was of no
assistance in the settlement of this problem, for, now that Dawson was mere consciousness only, the mirror gave back no
evidence of his material existence.

"This is awful!" he moaned, as he turned
and twisted his mind in a mad effort to
imagine how he looked. "Where in thun-
der can I have left myself?"

As he spoke the door opened, and a man
having the semblance of a valet entered.

"Good-morning, Mr. Dawson," said the
valet—for that is what the intruder was—
busying himself about the room. "I hope
you find yourself well this morning?"

"I can't find myself at all this morning!"
retorted Dawson. "What the devil does this
mean? Where's my body?"

"Which one, sir?" the valet inquired,
respectfully, pausing in his work.

"'GOOD-MORNING, MR. DAWSON'"

A Glance Ahead

"Which one?" echoed Dawson. "Wh—which— Oh, Lord! Excuse me, but how many bodies do I happen to have?" he added.

"Five—though a gentleman of your position, sir, ought to have at least ten, if I may make so bold as to speak, sir," said the valet. "Your golf body is pretty well used up, sir, you've played so many holes with it; and I really think you need a new one for evening wear, sir. The one you got from London is rather shabby, don't you think? It can't digest the simplest kind of a dinner, sir."

"The one I got from London, eh?" said Dawson. "I got a body in London, did I? And where's the one I got in Paris?" he demanded, sarcastically.

"You gave that to the coachman, sir," replied the valet. "It never fitted you, and, as you said yourself, it was rather gaudy, sir."

"Oh—I said that, did I? It was one of these loud, assertive, noisy bodies, eh?"

"Yes, sir, extremely so. None of your friends liked you in it, sir," said the valet. "Shall I fetch your lounging body, or will

you wish to go to church this morning?"
he continued.

"Bring 'em all in; bring every blessed
bone of 'em," said Dawson. "I want to
see how I look in 'em all; and bring me a
morning paper."

"A what, sir?" asked the valet, apparently somewhat perplexed by the order.

"A morning paper, you idiot!" retorted
Dawson, growing angry at the question.
The man seemed to be so very stupid.

"I don't quite understand what you wish,
sir," said the valet, apologetically.

"Oh, you don't, eh?" said Dawson,
amazed as well as annoyed at the man's
seeming lack of sense. "Well, I want to
read the news—"

"Ah! Excuse me, Mr. Dawson," said
the valet. "I did not understand. You
want the *Daily Ticker*."

"Oh, do I?" ejaculated Dawson. "Well,
if you know what I want better than I do,
bring me what you think I want, and add
to it a cup of coffee and a roll."

"I beg your pardon!" the valet returned.

"A cup of coffee and a roll!" roared Dawson. "Don't you know what a cup of

coffee and a roll is or are? Just ask the cook, will you—"

"Ask the what, sir?" asked the valet, very respectfully.

"The cook! the cook! the cook!" screamed Dawson. His patience was exhausted by such manifest dulness.

"I—I'm sincerely anxious to please you, Mr. Dawson," said his man; "but really, sir, you speak so strangely this morning, I hardly know what to do. I—"

"Can't you understand that I'm hungry?" demanded Dawson.

"Oh!" said the valet. "Hungry, of course; yes, you should be at this time in the morning; but—er—your bodies have already been refreshed, sir; I have attended to all that as usual."

"Ah! You've attended to all that, eh? And I've breakfasted, have I?"

"Your bodies have all been fed, sir," said the valet.

"Never mind me, then," said Dawson. "Bring in those well-fed figures of mine, and let me look at 'em. Meanwhile, turn on the—er—*Daily Ticker.*"

The valet bowed, walked across the

room, and touched a button on a board which had escaped Dawson's vigilant eye —possibly because his vigilant eye was elsewhere—and, with a sigh of perplexity, left the room. The response to the button pressure was immediate. A clicking as of a stock-ticker began to make itself heard, and from one corner of the bureau a strip of paper tape covered with letters of one kind and another emerged. Dawson watched it unfold for a moment, and then, approaching it, took in the types that were printed upon it. In an instant he understood a portion of the situation at least, although he did not wholly comprehend it. The date was December 25, 3568. He had gone to bed on Christmas eve, 1898. What had become of the intervening years he knew not—but this was undoubtedly the year of grace 3568, if the ticker was to be believed—and tickers rarely lie, as most stock-speculators know. Instead of living in the nineteenth century, Dawson had in some wise leaped forward into the thirty-sixth.

"Great Scott!" he cried. "Where have I been all this time? I don't wonder my poor old body is gone!"

A Glance Ahead

And then he started to peruse the news. The first item was a statement of governmental intent. It read something like a court circular.

"It is pleasant to announce on Christmas morning," he read, "that the business of the Administration has proven so successful during the year that all loyal citizens, on and after January 1, will be paid $10,000 a month instead of only $7600, as hitherto. The United States Railway Department, under the management of our distinguished Secretary of Railways, Mr. Hankinson Rawley, shows a profit of $750,-000,000,000 for the year. Mr. Johnneymaker, Secretary of Groceries, estimates the profits of his department at $600,000,000,-000, and the Secretary of War announces that the three highly successful series of battles between France and Germany held at the Madison Square Garden have netted the Treasury over $500,000 apiece — no doubt due to the fact that Emperor Bismarck XXXVII. and King Dreyfus XLVIII. led their troops in person. The showing of the Navy Department is quite as good. The good business sense of Secretary Smithers in securing the naval fights between Russia and the Anglo-Indians for American waters is fully established by the results. The twenty encounters between his Indo-Britannic Majesty's Arctic squadron and the Czar's Baltic fleet in Boston Harbor alone have cleared for our citizens $150,000,000 above the guarantees to the two belligerents; whereas the bombardment of St. Petersburg by the Anglo-Indians under our management, thanks to the efficient service of the Cook excursion-steamers direct to the scene of action, has brought us in several hundred millions more. It should be quite evident by this time that the Barnum & Bailey party have shown themselves worthy of the people's confidence."

Dawson forgot all about his possible bodily complications in reading this. Here was the United States gone into business, and instead of levying taxes was actually paying dividends. It was magnificent.

One might have thought that the unexpected announcement of the possession of an income of $120,000 a year would be sufficient to destroy any interest in whatever other news the *Ticker* might present; but with Dawson it only served to whet his curiosity, and he read on:

"The acquirement of the department stores by the government in 2433 has proven a decided success. Floorwalker-General Barker announces that the last of the bonds given in payment for the good-will of these institutions have matured and been paid off. This, too, out of the profits of four centuries. It is true that the laws requiring citizens to patronize these have helped much to bring about this desirable effect, and some credit for the present wholly satisfactory condition of affairs should be given to Senator Barca di Cinchona, of Peru, for having, in 2830, introduced the bill which for the time being covered him with execration. The profits for the coming year, on a conservative estimate, cannot be less than eighteen trillions of dollars—which, as our readers can see, will add much to the prosperity of the nation."

"Worse and worse!" cried Dawson. "Floorwalker-General—compulsory custom —eighteen trillions of dollars!" And then he read again:

"Over the Plum-Pudding"

"It will be with unexpected pleasure this Christmas morning, too, that our citizens will read the President's proclamation, in view of the unexampled prosperity of the past year, ordering a bonus of $15,000 gold to be delivered to every family in the land as a Christmas present from the Administration. This will relieve the vaults of the national Treasury of a store of coin that has been somewhat embarrassing to handle. The delivery-wagons will start on their rounds at six o'clock, and it is expected that by midday the money will have been wholly distributed. Residents of large cities are requested not to keep the carriers waiting at the door, since, as will be readily understood, the delivery of so much coin to so many millions of people is not an easy task. It is suggested that barrels of attested capacity be left on the walk, so that the coin may be placed into these without unnecessary delay. Those who still retain the old-fashioned coal-chutes can have the gold dumped into their cellars direct if they will simply have the covers to the coal-holes removed."

Dawson could hardly believe the announcement. Here was $15,000 coming to him this very morning. It was too good to be true, he thought; but the news was soon confirmed by the valet, who interrupted his reading by bursting breathlessly into the room.

"What on earth are we going to do, Mr. Dawson?" he cried. "The Christmas present has arrived. The cart is outside now."

"Do?" retorted Dawson. "Do? Why, get a shovel and shovel it in. What else?"

"That's easier said than done, sir," said the valet. "The gold-bin is chock-full already. You couldn't get a two-cent piece into the cellar, much less three thousand five-dollar gold pieces. They'd ought to have sent that money in certified checks."

Dawson experienced a sensation of mirth. The idea of quarrelling as to the form of a $15,000 gift struck him as being humorous.

"Isn't there any place but the gold-bin you can put it in?" he demanded. "How about the silver-bin, is that full?"

"I don't know what you mean by the silver-bin," replied the valet. "People don't use silver for money nowadays, sir."

"Oh, they don't, eh? And what do they do with it—pave streets?"

The valet smiled.

"You are having your little joke with me this morning, Mr. Dawson," he said, "or else you have forgotten that all we do with silver now is to make it into bricks and build houses with 'em."

"Well, I'll be hanged!" cried Dawson. "Really?"

"Certainly, sir," observed the valet. "You must remember how silver gradually cheapened and cheapened until finally it ruined the clay-brick industry?"

"Ah, yes," said Dawson. "I had temporarily forgotten. I do remember the tendency of silver to cheapen, but the ruin of the brick industry has escaped me. This house is—ah—built of silver bricks?"

"Of course it is, Mr. Dawson. As if you didn't know!" said the valet, with a deprecatory smirk.

"Ah—about how much coal—I mean gold—have we in the cellar?" Dawson asked.

"In eagles we have $230,000, sir, but I think there's half a million in fivers. I haven't counted up the $20 pieces for eight weeks, but I think we have a couple of tons left, sir."

"Then, James— Is your name James?"

"Yes, sir—James, or whatever else you please, sir," said the valet, accommodatingly.

"Then, James, if I have all that ready cash in the cellar, you can have the $15,000 that has just come. I—ah—I don't think I shall need it to-day," said Dawson, in a lordly fashion.

"Me, sir?" said James. "Thank you, sir, but really I have no place to put it. I don't know what to do with what I have already on hand."

"Then give it to the poor," said Dawson, desperately.

Again the valet smiled. He evidently thought his master very queer this morning.

"There ain't any poor any more, sir," he said.

"No poor?" cried Dawson.

"Of course not," said James. "Really, Mr. Dawson, you seem to have forgotten a great deal. Don't you remember how the forty-seventh amendment to the Constitution abolished poverty?"

"I—ah—I am afraid, James," said Dawson, gasping for breath, "that I've had a stroke of some kind during the night. All these things of which you speak seem—er—seem a little strange to me, James. There seems to be some lesion in my brain somewhere. Tell me about—er—how things are. Am I still in the United States?"

"Yes, sir, you are still in the United States."

"And the United States is bounded on the north by—"

"Sir, the United States has no northerly or southerly boundary. The Western Hemisphere is now the United States."

"And Europe?"

"Europe has not changed much since 1900, sir. Don't you remember how in the early years of the twentieth century the whole Eastern Hemisphere became European?"

"I remember that we took part in the division of China," said Dawson.

"Oh yes," said James, "quite so. But in 1920 don't you recall how we swapped off our share in China, together with the Dewey Islands, for Canada and all other British possessions on this side of the earth?"

"Dimly, James, only dimly," said Dawson, astonished, as well he might be, at the news, since he had never even imagined anything of the kind, although the Dewey Islands needed no explanation. "And we have ultimately acquired the whole hemisphere?"

"Yes, sir," replied James. "The South American republics came in naturally in 1940, and the Mexican War in 2363 ended, as it had to, in the conquest of Mexico."

"And, tell me, what are we doing with Patagonia?"

"One of the most flourishing States in the Union, Mr. Dawson. It was made the Immigrant State, sir. All persons immigrating to the United States, by an act of Congress passed in 2480, were compelled to go to Patagonia first, and forced to live there for a period of five years, studying American conditions, after which, provided they could pass an examination showing themselves equal to the duties of citizenship, they were permitted to go wherever else in the States they might choose."

"And suppose they couldn't pass?" Dawson asked.

"They had to stay in Patagonia until they could," said James. "It is known as the School of Instruction of the States. It is also our penal colony. Instead of prisons, we have a section of Patagonia set apart for the criminal element."

"And the negro?" asked Dawson. "How about him?"

"The negro, Mr. Dawson, if the histories say rightly, was an awful problem for a great many years. He had so many good points and so many bad that no one knew exactly what to do about him. Finally the sixty-third amendment was passed, ordering his deportation to Africa. It seemed like a hardship at first, but in 2863 he pulled himself together, and to-day has a continent of his own. Africa is his, and when nations are at war together they hire their troops from Africa. They make splendid soldiers, you know."

"What's become of Krüger and—er— Rhodes?" Dawson asked. "Turned black?"

A Glance Ahead

James laughed. "Oh, Rhodes and Krüger! Why, as I remember it, they smashed each other. But that is ancient history, Mr. Dawson."

"Jove!" cried Dawson. "What changes!" And then an idea crossed his mind. "James," said he, "pack up my luggage. We'll go to London."

"Where?" asked James.

"To the British capital," returned Dawson.

"Very well, sir," said James. "I will buy return tickets for Calcutta at once, sir. Shall we go on the 1.10 or the 3.40? The 1.10 is an express, but the 3.40 has a buffet."

"Which is the quicker?" Dawson asked.

"The 3.40 goes through in thirty-five minutes, sir. The 1.10 does it in half an hour."

"Great Scott!" said Dawson. "I think, on the whole, James, I won't try it until to-morrow. Calcutta, eh!" he added to himself. "James," he continued, "when did Calcutta become the British capital?"

"In 2964, sir," said James.

"And London?" queried Dawson.

"I don't know much about those island

towns, sir," said James. "It's said that London was once the British capital, but sensible people don't believe it much. Why, it hasn't more than twenty million inhabitants, mostly tailors."

"And how many citizens does a modern city have to have, to amount to anything, James?" asked Dawson, faintly.

"Well," said James scratching his head reflectively, "one hundred and sixty or two hundred millions, according to the last census."

"And New York reaches to where?" Dawson asked, in a tentative manner.

"Oh, not very far. It's only third, you know, in population. The last town annexed was Buffalo. The trouble with New York is that it has reached the limits of the State on every side. We'd make it bigger if we could, but Pennsylvania and Ohio and New Jersey won't give up an inch; and Canada is very jealous of her old boundaries."

"Wisely," said Dawson. And then he chose to be sarcastic. "Why don't they fill in the ocean with ashes and extend the city over the Atlantic, James? In an age

A Glance Ahead

of such marvellous growth so much waste space should be utilized," he said.

"Oh, it is," returned the valet. "You, of course, know that all the West Indies are now connected by means of a cinder-track with the mainland?"

"And is the bicycle-path to the Azores built yet?" demanded Dawson, dryly.

"No, Mr. Dawson," replied James. "That was given up in 2947, when the patent balloon tires were invented, by means of which wheelmen can scorch wherever they choose to through space, irrespective of roads."

Dawson gasped. "For Heaven's sake, James," he cried, "I need air! Bring up the bodies, and let me get aboard one of 'em and take a sleigh-ride in Central Park. I can't stand this much longer."

The valet laughed heartily.

"Sleigh-rides have gone out in the Central Park, sir. When Mr. Bunkerton started his earth-heating-and-cooling plant snow was practically abolished hereabouts, Mr. Dawson," said he. "It's never cold enough for snow — always about seventy degrees."

"Over the Plum-Pudding"

"Ah! The earth is heated from a central station, eh?" asked Dawson.

"Heated and cooled, sir. What with the hot and cold air running through flues from Vesuvius and the north pole into a central reservoir, an absolute mean temperature that never varies from one year's end to another has been obtained. If you wish to take a sleigh-ride you'll have to go to Mars, sir, and just at present the ships running both ways are crowded. They always are during the holiday season. I doubt if you could secure passage for a week."

"Bring up the bodies!" roared Dawson. "I can't express myself in this disembodied state. Mean temperature everywhere; income provided by government; no taxes; no poor; gold dumped into the cellar; houses built of silver; sleigh-riding at Mars. *Bring up the bodies!* Do you hear? The mere idea is wrecking my mind. Give me something physical, and give it to me quick."

Dawson's emotion was so overpowering that the valet was really frightened, and he fled below, whence he shortly reappeared, pushing before him a small wheeling vehicle in which sat three villanous-looking bodies,

"THREE VILLANOUS-LOOKING BODIES, AND A FOURTH, WHICH
DAWSON RECOGNIZED AS HIS OWN"

and a fourth, which Dawson, with a gasp of relief, recognized as his own.

"I thought you said I had five of these things?" he demanded, inspecting the bodies.

"So you have, sir. The one you wear for evening, sir, is being pressed. You fell asleep in it the other night, sir, and got it all wrinkled."

"That golf fellow's a gay-looking prig!" laughed Dawson. "Let me try him on."

The valet stood the body up, and, opening a small door at the top of the skull, ingeniously concealed by the hair, invited Dawson to enter. Without even knowing how it came about, Dawson soon found himself in full possession. Then he walked over to the glass and peered in at himself.

"Humph!" he said. "Not much to look at, am I? Bring me a driver."

James obeyed, and Dawson tried the swing.

"Why, the darned thing's left-handed!" he said, after some awkward work. "I don't like that."

"You picked it out for yourself, sir," replied the valet. "You said a left-handed player always rattled the other man, and, besides, it was the only one you ever had that could keep its eye on the ball."

"Let me out! Let me out!" screamed Dawson. "I don't like it, and I won't have it. I'm suffocating. Open my head and let me out."

The valet unfastened the little door, and Dawson emerged. "What's that tough-looking one for?" he asked, after a pause, during which his brain throbbed with the excitement of his novel experience.

"Prize-fights," said James.

"And the strange-looking thing that appears to have been designed for a fancy-dress ball?"

"Nobody knows what you intended that for, Mr. Dawson. You had it sent up yourself from the bodydasher's last week, sir."

"Well, take it away," roared Dawson. "This may be 3568, but I haven't lost my self-respect entirely. Give it to—ah—give it to the children to play with."

"Really, Mr. Dawson," said the valet, anxiously, "wouldn't I better ring up the President and have him send a doctor here from the Department of Physic? You seem all astray this morning. There aren't any children any more, sir."

"Wha — what? No *children?*" cried Dawson.

"They were abolished three centuries ago, sir," explained the valet.

"Then how the deuce is the world populated?" demanded Dawson.

"It was sufficiently populated at the time the law abolishing children was passed, sir."

"But people die, don't they?"

"Never," replied the valet. "When Dr. Perkinbloom discovered how to separate man's mental from his physical side, by means of this little door in the cranium, all the perishable portions of man were done away with, which is how it is, sir, that, for convenience' sake, after the world was as full of consciousness as it could be comfortably, it was decided not to have any more of it."

"But these bodies, James—these bodies?"

"Oh, they are manufactured—"

"But how?"

"That, sir, is the secret of the inventor," replied the valet, "a secret which he is permitted by our government to retain, although the factories are maintained under the supervision of the Tailor-General."

Dawson was silent. He was absolutely overpowered by the revelation.

"James," he said, after a pause of nearly five minutes, "let me—let me back into my old self just for a moment, please. I—I feel faint, and sort of uncomfortable. I feel lost, don't you know. I can grasp some of your ideas, but—Christmas without children! It does not seem possible."

The valet respectfully raised up the original Dawson, opened the little door in the top of its head, and Dawson slipped in.

"Now lock that door," said Dawson, quickly, once he was safe inside. The valet obeyed nervously.

"Give me the key," said Dawson. "Quick!"

"Yes, sir," said James, handing it over, eying his master anxiously meanwhile.

Dawson looked at it. It was a fragile bit of gold, but gold did not appeal to him at the moment, and before the valet could interfere to stop him he had hurled it far out of the window into the busy street below, where it was lost in the maze of traffic.

"There," said Dawson; "I guess you'll have a hard time getting me out of this again. You needn't try. And meanwhile, James, you can kick those other bodies out into the street and dump the gold into the river; after which you may present my compliments to your darned old government, and tell it that it can go where the woodbine twineth. A government that abolishes children can go hang, so far as I am concerned."

James sprang towards Dawson as if he had been stung. His face grew white with wrath.

"Sir," he hissed, passionately, "the words that you have spoken are treason, and merit punishment."

"What's that?" cried Dawson, wrathfully.

"Treason is what I said," retorted the valet, aroused. "If I thought you were in your right mind and knew what you were saying, I should conduct you forthwith to the police-station and inform against you to the Secretary of Justice."

"Over the Plum-Pudding"

"Get out of here, you—you—you impertinent ass!" cried Dawson. "Leave the room! I—I—I discharge you! You forget your position!"

"It is you who forget your position," returned the valet. "Discharge me! I like that. You might just as well try to discharge the President of the United States as me."

Here the valet gave a scornful laugh, and leered maddeningly at Dawson. The latter gazed at him coldly.

"You are my servant?" he demanded.

"By government appointment, at your service," replied James, with a satirical bow. "You have overlooked the fact that the government since 1900 has gradually absorbed all business—every function of labor is now governmental—and a man who arbitrarily bounces a cook, as the ancients used to put it, strikes at the administration. Charges may be preferred against a servant, but he cannot be deprived of his office except upon the report of a committee to the Department of Intelligence. As the President is your servant, so am I."

A Glance Ahead

Dawson sat down aghast, and clutched his forehead with his hands.

"But," he cried, jumping to his feet, "that is intolerable. The logic of the thing makes you, while your party is in power—"

"Your governor," interrupted the valet. "Come," he added, firmly. "You called me an impertinent ass a moment ago, and my patience is exhausted. I shall inform against you. If you aren't sent to Patagonia before night, my name is not James Wilkins."

He laid his hand on Dawson's shoulder roughly. A shock, as of electricity, went through Dawson's person. His old-time strength returned to him, and, turning viciously upon the impudent fellow, he grasped him about his middle with both arms, and, after a struggle that lasted several minutes, dragged him to the window and hurled him, even as he had the key, down into the street below.

This done, he fell unconscious to the floor.

A year has passed since the episode, and Dawson has become the happiest man in the world, for on his return to consciousness, instead of finding himself in the hands of a revengeful valet, backed by a socialistic government, the past had been restored to him and the future relegated to its proper place. It was only the other night that he spoke of the value of his experience, however.

"It has made me happier, in spite of my many troubles," he said. "If there's anything that can make the present endurable it is the thought of what the future may have in store for us. A guaranteed income, and a detachable spirit, and no taxes, and a variety of imperishable bodies are all very nice, but servants with the manners of custom-house officials, and children abolished! No, thank you. Curious dream, though," he added, "don't you think?"

"No," said I, "not very. It strikes me as a reasonable forecast of what is likely to be if things keep on as they are going. Especially in that matter of our servants."

"Maybe it wasn't a dream," said Dawson. "Maybe, time having neither beginning nor ending, the future is, and I stumbled into it."

A Glance Ahead

"Maybe so," said I. "I think, however, you'll have some difficulty in finding that $15,000 again."

"I don't want to," observed Dawson. "For don't you see I'd find James Wilkins's dead body beside it, and, in spite of its drawbacks, I prefer life in New York to the possibility of Patagonia."

Hans Pumpernickel's Vigil

Hans Pumpernickel's Vigil

HANS PUMPERNICKEL was for many years regarded by his friends and neighbors in the little town of Schnitzelhammerstein - on - the Zugvitz as the most industrious boy they had ever known. Where Hans came from no one knew. He had appeared in Schnitzelhammerstein-on-the-Zugvitz when he was not more than six years old. His name was all that he would confide to the curious.

"I'm Hans Pumpernickel," he had answered, in response to the inquiries of the inquisitive. "But where I came from is neither here nor there."

Some said that this statement was only half true, though many others believed it wholly. Certain it is, however, that if one has a hailing-place, a native town, it must be either here or there. If it is not here, it must be there, said some; but Hans never took the trouble to say anything further on the subject.

"And what are you going to do to live?" asked the Mayor's wife, who took a great interest in the pretty little stranger when first she saw him.

"Breathe," said Hans, simply. "For you see, ma'am, I cannot live without breathing, and so I have decided to do that."

The Mayor said that this was impudence; but the good lady, who had made that somewhat crabbed old person's life more happy than he deserved, only laughed, and said that she thought it was droll, and only wished her little boy, who was stupid like his father, could have said something as bright.

"But you cannot breathe unless you eat," the Mayor's wife had said, when Hans had spoken. "What are you going to eat?"

"I do not know," said Hans. "What have you got?"

Again the Mayor growled "Impudence!" and again did the good lady laugh.

"We have sausages and cake and apples," she said.

Hans Pumpernickel's Vigil

"Then," said Hans, "I will have some sausages and cake and apples."

"But we don't give away things of that kind," said the lady. "Those who would eat must work."

"I cannot work unless I breathe," said Hans; "and you yourself have said that I cannot breathe unless I eat. Therefore, if you would have me work, you must let me eat."

"Logic!" cried the Mayor, beginning to take an interest in Hans. "Give the boy an apple."

So Hans was given the apple, and he ate it so thoroughly that the Mayor decided that he was just the boy to do little errands for him, for thoroughness was a quality he greatly admired, and from that time on Hans lived in the Mayor's family; and when the stupid little son of that exalted personage ran away from home and became a cabin-boy on a man-of-war, the Mayor adopted Hans, and he took the place of the boy who had gone away, refusing, however, much to the Mayor's sorrow, to change his name from Pumpernickel to Ehrenbreitstein, which happened to be the last name of the Mayor.

"Over the Plum-Pudding"

"Pumpernickel was I born," said Hans, "and Pumpernickel will I remain. Why should I, a Pumpernickel who am bound to make a name for myself sooner or later, take the name of some one else, and shed the lustre of my fame upon *his* family?"

All of which was very sensible, though Mayor Ehrenbreitstein did not appreciate that fact.

So Hans went on making himself very useful to the Mayor and his wife. He would shell pease in the morning for the Lady Mayor, and in the afternoon he would write speeches for the Mayor to deliver on public occasions; and people said that as a public speaker the Mayor was improving, while all who had the pleasure of dining with the head of the city frequently complimented the Lady Mayor upon the excellence of the pease served at her banquets. In every way was Hans satisfactory to all for whom he worked. After a while such confidence did he inspire in his employers that Frau Ehrenbreitstein let him do all her shopping for her, and most of the Mayor's duties were intrusted to the boy. He could match

Hans Pumpernickel's Vigil

ribbons and veto or approve the doings of
the aldermen of Schnitzelhammerstein-on-
the-Zugvitz with equal perfection. The
ribbons he matched and the worsteds he
chose for his kind mistress always looked
well, and the lady soon became in the
popular estimation a person of unusually
good taste, while the vetoes and other public
papers were so well phrased that even his
opponents were forced to admit that the
magistrate was right.

Hans bore all his prosperity with modesty,
and for the fifteen years during which he
faithfully served his employers he developed
no conceit whatsoever, as many a weaker
boy might reasonably have done, and, bar-
ring one peculiarity, none of the eccentricities
of the truly great ever manifested themselves. This one peculiarity excited much
curiosity among those who had heard of it,
but despite all questionings Hans declined
to say why he had it. It was a peculiarity
that was indeed peculiar. It was noticed
that from the time he first ate with the family of the Mayor he would set apart one full
third of every dainty that was placed upon
his plate, and when the meal was over he

would take it away from the table rolled
up in a napkin. For instance, if at break-
fast three sausages fell to the lot of Hans,
he would eat two of them, and the third
he would wrap up in a napkin, and take it
to his room. So it was with everything else
that came his way. Out of every three
apples one would go untouched into the
napkin; and later, when he began to earn
a little money, one-third of it also would
be saved. It was noticed, too, that on every
Friday afternoon Hans would send away
a big box by the express carrier, but to whom
the box was sent no one could learn. The
express carrier would not tell, and Hans
himself, when asked about it, would say
to the one who asked him:

"Let me see. You are in what business?"

"I am a baker," or, perhaps, "I am a
butcher," the inquisitive one would say.

"Then," said Hans, "if I were you, I
would stick to baking or to butching, and
not embark on enterprises which are not
allied to the making of bread or the slaugh-
ter of roast beef."

The people so addressed would turn away
chagrined, but with proper apologies; and

when they apologized Hans would say, with a smile, "Pray don't mention it," so kindly that the meddlers would be pacified, and no ill feeling ever resulted from the young boy's request that they mind their own business.

At the end of the fifteen years of faithful work, however, a great change seemed to come over Hans. He began to show a great distaste for the labors that he had hitherto spent his time in performing. When Frau Ehrenbreitstein gave him a skein of pink zephyr to take to town to match, he would try to beg off, and when he could not beg off he did worse. He went to town and brought back, not the new skein of pink zephyr that his mistress wanted, but a roll of green and yellow wall-paper, and, when she expressed surprise, he said that that was the best he could do.

"But I didn't want wall-paper," cried the Lady Mayor.

"Well, you never told me that," said Hans. "You said, I admit, that you wanted pink zephyr; but then one might wish for that and still want a roll of green and yellow wall-paper."

145

"Over the Plum-Pudding"

"Are you crazy?" returned the good lady, much mystified.

"I think not; and the mere fact that I *think* not shows that I am not," Hans replied, "for the very good reason that if I had lost my mind I could not think at all."

"Very well," said Frau Ehrenbreitstein, reassured by this perfectly logical answer. "You may go and shell the pease."

Whereupon Hans went down into the kitchen and shelled the pease, only he retained the pods this time, and threw the pease to the pigs.

"It is very evident to me," observed his good mistress to her husband that night, when the pods were served at dinner, "that Hans Pumpernickel has something on his mind."

"Yes, my dear," answered the Mayor. "I know he has, and I know what it is."

"He is not in love, I hope?" said Frau Ehrenbreitstein.

"Not he!" cried the Mayor. "He is thinking about what I shall say to the Emperor next week when his Imperial Majesty and the Chancellor pass through Schnitzel-hammerstein - on - the - Zugvitz on their

Hans Pumpernickel's Vigil

way to the Schutzenfest at Würtemburger-Darmstadt. I have told Hans that the imperial train stops at our station to water the engine, and during the five minutes or so in which the Emperor honors our burg with his presence it is only fitting that I, as Lord Mayor, should greet him with an address of welcome. It will be the opportunity of my life, and the boy is trying to enable me to be equal to it. Heaven forbid that he should fail!''

This explanation eased the mind of the Mayor's wife, and she refrained from asking Hans to shell pease and match zephyrs until after the Emperor had come and gone. Unfortunately, however, this was not the real cause of the trouble with Hans, as the speech he wrote for the Mayor to deliver to his imperial master showed; for, to the dismay of Mayor Ehrenbreitstein, when the Emperor's train stopped at Schnitzelhammerstein-on-the-Zugvitz, and he had unrolled the address Hans had written, he discovered that Hans had not written a speech at all, but a comic poem, in which his Imperial Majesty was referred to as a royal turkey-cock, with a crow like the squeak of a penny flute. The poor Mayor nearly expired when his eyes rested on the lines Hans had written; but he went bravely ahead and made up a speech of his own, which his Majesty fortunately did not hear, owing to the noise made by the steam escaping from the engine whistle.

When the Emperor had departed, the Mayor returned home in a rage, and you may be sure that Hans could not get in a word edgewise even until his employer had told him what he thought of him.

"Excuse me," said Hans, when the Mayor had finished, after an hour's angry tirade—"excuse me, but would you mind saying that over again? I was thinking of something else."

"Say it over again?" shrieked the Mayor. "Never. I shall never speak to you again."

"But what have I done?" asked Hans, so innocently that the Mayor relented and repeated his tirade, and then Hans broke down.

"Did I do that?" he said. "Then it is very plain that I need a vacation."

"I think so," retorted the Mayor. "You may take the next thousand years without pay."

"HE'S THE WORST BABY YOU EVER SAW"

Hans Pumpernickel's Vigil

"One year will be sufficient," said Hans. "Though I thank you just as kindly for the others." Then he wept, and the Mayor's wife took pity on him, and asked him to tell her what it was that had so occupied his mind of late that he had committed so many grievous errors, and Hans told her all.

"It's my great - great - great - great - great-granduncle's fault," he sobbed.

"Your what?" cried his mistress.

"My great - great - great - great - great - granduncle, the perpetual baby," said Hans, wiping his eyes. "He's the worst baby you ever saw. He yells and howls and howls and yells all the time, and if he is left alone or put down for a moment he has a convulsion of rage that is terrible to witness. He breaks his toys the minute he gets them, and for fifteen years he has made a slave of my poor father, who has not let the child out of his lap in all that time."

"Fifteen years?" cried Frau Ehrenbreitstein. "What *do* you mean? How old is this baby?"

"Three hundred and forty-seven years, six months, and eight days," said Hans,

149

ruefully, consulting a pocket calendar he had with him. "During my time with you," he added, "I have supported them. Father is alone in the house with the infant; we could not afford a servant, and the child yells so all the time that my father cannot get employment anywhere. It was this that drove me out into the world to earn a living for them. When I got only my food and bed, I shared my food with them, sending off a third of it every week. Then when money came along, I gave them a third of that; but the baby is as bad as ever, and father has written to say that he can stand it no more, and I must return home or he will send the baby to me here."

"But, mercy me!" roared the Mayor, who had come in and heard the story, "why doesn't the child grow?"

"He can't," sobbed Hans. "His mother once made a wish that he might always remain a baby, and it happened that she made the wish at the one instant of the year when all wishes are granted by the fairies."

"Nonsense," said the Mayor. "There are no fairies."

"IT WAS A WEARY VIGIL, BUT HE WAS TRUE"

Hans Pumpernickel's Vigil

"Indeed, there are," said Hans. "There is my great - great - great - great - great - granduncle, the baby, to prove it. He's a little tyrant, and he has worn out every generation of the family since, making them look after him. It's terrible, and in trying to think what to do to relieve my poor father and still support myself I have neglected everything else, and that is why I—boo-hoo!—I wrote the wall-paper and matched a pink Emperor with a green and yellow comic poem."

"Poor lad!" said the Mayor's wife. "Poor lad! It is a cruel story."

"It is that," agreed the Mayor. "But cheer up, Hans. If there is an instant in every year when wishes are always granted by the fairies, why don't you wish the baby as he ought to be at the right moment?"

"That's the trouble," said Hans, sadly. "There are many instants in a year, and the lucky moment changes every twelve months. It is never the same. I wish, and *wish*, but never at the right moment. Sometimes I forget it ; the instant comes and is gone, though I don't know it."

"Well," said the Mayor's wife, "there

"Over the Plum-Pudding"

is but one thing you can do. That is, to devote a whole year to nothing else but that wish. I shall fix you up a chair in the kitchen, give you a pipe, and on New-Year's morning you may begin. You shall have no other duties but to wish for a restoration of things as they should be. You will be sure to hit the right moment if you are faithful to your work."

"As I always am," said Hans, drying his tears.

And so it was that Hans Pumpernickel began his long vigil. He sat in the kitchen, silent, smoking, gazing at the ceiling, wishing. It was weary work indeed, but he was true, and last year, on the sixteenth day of July, at half-past one o'clock in the morning, his fidelity was rewarded, though he did not know it until the next morning, when the expressman brought him a message from his father to the following effect:

" *July* 16, 1893.

"MY DEAR HANS,—Don't worry; everything is serene again. At half-past one o'clock this morning, just as the clock struck, your great-great-great-great-great-granduncle began to grow at a most rapid pace. I had hardly time to drop him when he was taller than

Hans Pumpernickel's Vigil

I, and twice as stout as I am told you are. A beard
sprouted on his face with equal rapidity, and, just
as I thought to ask him what he was going to do next,
he gave a deafening shout of laughter and disappeared entirely. The whole affair didn't last more
than five seconds. The spell has been removed, and
the perpetual baby is no more. Come over and see
me, and we'll celebrate our emancipation.

" Affectionately your daddy,
" RUPERT PUMPERNICKEL."

Hans read this letter with a joyful face,
and rushed up-stairs to tell the Mayor and
his faithful helpmate of his good fortune,
and there was great rejoicing for several
days. Then Hans visited his father, and
the two happy creatures spent weeks and
weeks rambling contentedly about the
country together, at the end of which time
Hans returned to Schnitzelhammerstein-
on-the-Zugvitz, where, the Emperor having
retired the Mayor on a liberal pension for
his attentions and kind expressions of regard in the speech Hans did not write for
him, he was chosen to succeed his former
master.

The Affliction of Baron Humpfelhimmel

The Affliction of Baron Humpfelhimmel

EVERYBODY said it was an extraordinary affair altogether, and for once everybody was right. Baron Humpfelhimmel himself would say nothing about it for two reasons. The first reason was that nobody dared ask him what he thought about it, and the second was that he was too proud to speak to anybody concerning any subject whatsoever, unless questioned. That he always laughed, no matter what happened, was the melancholy fact, and had been a melancholy fact from his childhood's earliest hour. He was born laughing. He laughed in church, he laughed at home. When his father spanked him he roared with laughter, and when he suffered from the measles he could not begin to restrain his mirth.

The situation seemed all the more sin-

gular when it was remembered that Rudolf
von Pepperpotz, the previous Baron Humpfelhimmel, and father of the Laughing
Baron, as he was called, was never known
to smile from his childhood's earliest hour
to his dying day, and, strangest of all,
was a far more amiable person, despite his
solemnity, than the present Baron for all
his laughter.

"What does it mean, do you suppose?"
Frau Ehrenbreitstein once asked of Hans
Pumpernickel, her husband's private secretary, of whom you have already had some
account.

"I cannot tell," Hans had answered,
"and I have my reason for saying that I
cannot tell," he added, significantly.

"What is that reason, Hans?" asked
the good lady, her curiosity aroused by the
boy's manner.

"It is this," said Hans, his voice sinking
to a whisper. "I cannot tell, because—because I do not know!"

And this, let me say in passing, was why
Hans Pumpernickel was thought by all to
be so wise. He had a reason always for
what he did, and was ever willing to give it.

Affliction of Baron Humpfelhimmel

"They say," the good Lady Ehrenbreit-stein went on—"they do say that when last winter the Baron while hunting boars was thrown from his horse, breaking his leg and two of his ribs, they could not be set because of his convulsions of laughter, though for my part I cannot see wherein having one's leg and ribs broken is provocative of merriment."

"Nor I," quoth Hans. "I have an eye for jokes. In most things I can see the fun, but in the breaking of one's bones I see more cause for tears than smiles."

And it was true. As Frau Ehrenbreit-stein had heard, the Baron Humpfelhimmel had broken one leg and two ribs—only it was while hunting wolves and not in a boar chase—and when the Emperor's physician, who was one of the party, came to where the suffering man lay he found him roaring with laughter.

"Good!" cried the physician, leaning over his prostrate form. "I am glad to see that you are not hurt. I feared you were injured."

"I am injured," the Baron replied, with a loud laugh. "My left leg — ha - ha-ha!—is nearly killing me—hee-hee!—with

p-pain, and if I mistake not, either my heart
—ha-ha-ha-ha!—or my ribs—hee-hee-hee!
—are broken in nineteen places."

Then he went off into such an explosion
of mirth as not only appeared unseemly,
but also deprived him of the power of speech
for five or six minutes.

"I fail to see the joke," said the physician, as the Baron's laughter echoed and
reechoed throughout the forest.

"Th-there—hee-hee!—there isn't a-any
joke," the Baron answered, smiling. "Con-
found you — ha-ha-ha-ha! — oho-ho-ho! —
can't you see I'm suffering?"

"I see you are laughing," the physician
replied—"laughing as if you were reading
a comic paper full of real jokes. What are
you laughing at?"

"Ha-ha! I—I d-dud-don't know," stam-
mered the Baron, vainly endeavoring to
suppress his mirth. "I—I don't feel like
laughing—hee-hee!—but I can't help it."
And off he went into another gale. Nor
did he stop there. The physician tried
vainly to quiet him down so that he could
set the fractured bones, but in spite of all
he could do for him the Baron either would

not or could not stop laughing. When he was able to move about again it was only with a limp, and even that appeared to have its humorous side, for whenever the Baron appeared on the public streets he was always smiling, and when the Mayor ventured to express his sympathy with him over his misfortune the Baron laughed again, and mirthfully requested him to mind his own business.

Then it was recalled how that ten years before, when the famous Von Pepperpotz Castle was destroyed by fire, the Baron was found writing in his study by the messenger who brought the news.

"Baron," the messenger cried—"Baron, the château is burning. The flames have already destroyed the armory, and are now eating their way through the corridors to the state banquet-hall."

The Baron looked the messenger in the eye for an instant, and then his face wreathed with smiles.

"My castle's burning, eh? Ha-ha-ha!" was what he said; and then, rising hurriedly from his desk, he hastened, shouting with laughter, to the scene, where no one worked harder than he to stay the devastating course of the flames.

"You seem to be pleased," said one who noticed his merriment.

The Baron's answer was a blow which knocked the fellow down, and then, striking him across the shoulders with his staff, he walked away, muttering to himself:

"Pleased! Ha-ha-ha! Does ruin please anybody—tee-hee-hee! If the churls only —tee-hee!—only knew—ha-ha-ha-ha!"

That was it! If they only knew! And no one did know until after the Baron had died without children—for he had never married — and all his possessions and papers became the property of the state. Through these papers the secret of the Baron's laughter became known to the good people of Schnitzelhammerstein-on-the-Zugvitz, and through them it became known to me. Hans Pumpernickel himself told me the tale, and as he has risen to the exalted position of Mayor of Schnitzelhammerstein-on-the-Zugvitz, an honor conferred only on the truly good and worthy, I have no reason to doubt that the story is in every way truthful.

"'MY CASTLE'S BURNING, EH? HA-HA!'"

Affliction of Baron Humpfelhimmel

"When Baron Humpfelhimmel died," said Hans, as he and I walked together along the beautiful sylvan path that runs by the side of the Zugvitz River, "I am sorry to say there were few mourners. A man who laughs, as a rule, is popular, but the man who laughs always, without regard to circumstances, makes enemies. One learns to love a person who laughs at one's jests, but one who laughs at funerals, at conflagrations, at beggars, at the needy and the distressed, does not become universally beloved. Such was the habit of Fritz von Pepperpotz, last of the Barons Humpfelhimmel. If you were to go to him with a funny story, none would laugh more heartily than he; but equally loud would he laugh were you to say to him that you had a racking headache, and should it chance that you were to inform him you had been desperately ill, his mirth would know no bounds. Even in his greatest frenzies of rage he would smirk and laugh, and so it happened that the popularity which you would expect would go with a mirthful disposition was the last thing in the world he could hope for. I do

"Over the Plum-Pudding"

not exaggerate when I say that Baron
Humpfelhimmel could not have been elected
office-boy to the Mayor on a popular vote,
even if there were no opposing candidate.
Now that it is all over, however, and we
know the truth, we have changed our minds
about it, and already several hundred of our
citizens have raised a fund of twenty marks
to go towards putting up a monument to
the memory of the Laughing Baron.

"Fritz von Pepperpotz, my friend," said
Hans to me, in explanation of the situation,
"laughed because he could not help it, as a
statement found among his papers after he
died showed. The statement contained the
whole story, and in some of its details it is
a sad one. It was all the fault of the grandfather of the late Baron that he could do
nothing but laugh all his days, that he
died unmarried, and that the name of Von
Pepperpotz has died off the face of the earth
forever, unless some one else chooses to as-
sume that name, which, I imagine, no one
is crazy enough to do. The only thing
that could reconcile me to such a name
would be the estates that formerly went
with it, but now that they have become the

property of the government the house has lost all of its attractions, retaining, however, every bit of its homeliness. Pumpernickel is bad enough, but it is beautiful beside Von Pepperpotz."

Here Hans sighed, and to comfort him, rather than to say anything I really meant, I observed that I thought Pumpernickel was a good strong name.

"Yes," Hans said, with a pleased smile. "It certainly is strong. I have had mine twenty-five years now, and it doesn't show the slightest sign of wear. It's as good as the day it was made, But to return to the Von Pepperpotz family and its mysterious affliction.

"According to the Baron's statement, while he himself could not restrain his mirth, no matter how badly he felt, his father, Rupert von Pepperpotz, could never smile, although he was a man of most genial disposition. Just as Fritz was ushered into the world, grinning like a Cheshire cheese—"

"Cat," I suggested, noting Hans's error.

"Cat, is it?" he said. "Well, now, do

"Over the Plum-Pudding"

you know I am glad to hear that? I always supposed the term used was cheese, and positively I have lain awake night after night trying to comprehend how a cheese could grin, and finally I gave it up, setting it down as one of the peculiarities of the English language. If it's Cheshire cat, and not Cheshire cheese, why, it's all clear as a pikestaff. But, as I was saying, just as Fritz was born grinning like a Cheshire cat, his father Rupert was born frowning apparently with rage. He was the most ill-natured-looking baby you ever saw, according to the chronicles. Nothing seemed to please him. When you or I would have cooed, Rupert von Pepperpotz would wrinkle up his forehead until the furrows, if his nurse tells the truth, were deep enough to hide letters in.

"And yet he was rarely cross, and never disobedient. It was the strangest thing in the world. Here was a being who always frowned and never laughed, and yet who was as obliging in his actions as could be. As he grew older his active amiability increased, but his frown grew more terrible than ever. He became a great wit. As

"RUPERT WAS ALWAYS MERRY"

Affliction of Baron Humpfelhimmel

he walked through the streets of Schnitzelhammerstein-on-the-Zugvitz he was always merry, though none would have
guessed it to look at him. He had a pleasant voice, and his neighbors all said it was
a most startling thing to hear in the distance a jolly, roistering song, and then to
walk along a little way and see that it was
this forbidding-looking person who was doing the singing.

"How Rupert got Wilhelmina de Grootz-
enburg to become his wife, considering
his seeming solemnity, which made him
appear to be positively ugly, nobody ever
knew. It is probable, however, that it
was sympathy which moved her to like him,
unless it was that his ugliness fascinated
her. Rupert himself said that it was not
sympathy for his inability to laugh or smile,
because he did not want sympathy for that.
He didn't feel badly about it himself. He
never had smiled, and so did not know
the pleasure of it. Consequently he didn't
miss it. Smiling was an idiotic way of
expressing pleasure anyhow, he said. Why
just because a man thought of a funny
idea he should stretch his mouth he couldn't

see. No more could he understand why it was necessary to show one's appreciation of a funny story by shaking one's stomach and saying Ha-ha! On the whole, he said that he was satisfied. He could talk and could tell people he enjoyed their stories without having to shake himself or disturb the corners of his mouth. When little Fritz was born, and did nothing but laugh even when he had the colic, the solemn-looking Rupert observed that the baby simply proved the truth of what he said.

"'What a donkey the child is,' he cried, 'to spoil his pretty face by stretching his mouth so that you almost fear his ears will drop into it! And those wild whoops, which you call laughter, what earthly use are they? I can't see why, if he is glad about something, he can't just say, "I'm glad about so and so," mildly, instead of making me deaf with his roars. Truly, laughter is not what it is cracked up to be.'

"'Ah, my dear Rupert,' Wilhelmina, his wife, had said, 'you do not really know what you are talking about! If you could enjoy the sensation of laughing once you would never wish to be without it.'

Affliction of Baron Humpfelhimmel

"'Nonsense!' replied the Baron. 'My father never laughed, so why should I wish to?'

"Now, then," continued Hans, "according to Fritz von Pepperpotz's statement, there was where Rupert was wrong. Siegfried von Pepperpotz had known what it was to laugh, but he had not known when to laugh, which was why the family of Von Pepperpotz was afflicted with a curse, which only the final dying out of the family could remove, and there lay the solution of the mystery. It seems that Siegfried von Pepperpotz, grandfather of Fritz and father of Rupert, had been a wild sort of a youth, who smiled when he wished and frowned when he wished, no matter what the occasion may have been, and he smiled once too often. A miserable-looking figure of a man once passed through the village of Schnitzelhammerstein-on-the-Zugvitz, selling sugar dolls and other sweets. To Siegfried and his comrades it seemed good to play a prank on the old fellow. They sent him two miles off into the country, where, they said, was a rich countess, who would buy his whole stock, when in reality there was no rich countess there at all, so that the old man had his trouble for his pains.

"That he was a magician they did not know, but so he was, and in those days magicians could do everything. Of course he was angry at the deception, and on his return to Schnitzelhammerstein-on-the-Zugvitz he sent for the young men, and got all of them to apologize and buy his wares except Siegfried. Siegfried not only refused to apologize and buy the old man's candies, but had the audacity to laugh in his face, and tell him about a wealthy old duke who lived two miles out on the other side of the village, which the magician immediately recognized as another attempt to play a practical joke upon him.

"'Enough, Siegfried von Pepperpotz!' he cried, in his rage. 'Laugh away while you can. After to-day may you never smile, and may your son never smile, and may your son's son, willing or unwilling, smile smiles that you two would have smiled, and so may it ever go! May every third generation get the laughter that the preceding two shall lose, according to my curse!'

"SIEGFRIED VON PEPPERPOTZ GREW ILL OF IT"

"This made Siegfried laugh all the harder, for, not knowing, as I have said, that the old man was a magician, he had no fear of him. Next day, however, he changed his mind. He found that he could not laugh. He could not even smile. Try as he would, his lips refused to do his bidding.

"It ruined his disposition. Siegfried von Pepperpotz grew ill over it. The greatest doctors in the world were summoned to his aid, but to no avail. If the curse had ended with him he might not have minded it so much, but after the discovery that from the day of his birth his son Rupert was no more able to laugh than himself he began to brood over the affliction, and shortly died of it; and when Fritz found out from a paper he discovered in a secret drawer in the old chest in the château what the curse was—for Siegfried never told his son, and alone knew from what it was he suffered, and that it was perpetual—he resolved that there should be no further posterity to whom it should be handed down.

"That," said Hans, "is the story of Baron Humpfelhimmel's affliction."

"And a strange story it is," said I.

"Over the Plum-Pudding"

"Though I don't know that it has any particular moral."

"Oh yes, it has!" said Hans. "It has a good moral."

"And what is that?" I asked.

"Don't laugh at your own jokes," he replied. "If Siegfried von Pepperpotz had not laughed when the magician came back, he never would have been cursed, and this story never would have been told."

A Great Composer

A Great Composer

MONG the best-known residents of Schnitzelhammerstein - on - the-Zugvitz when Hans Pumpernickel first appeared in that beautiful city were three musicians — Herr von Kärlingtongs, who was the only, and consequently the best, violinist in town, Dr. Otto Teutonstring, and Heinrich Flatz, who had played the 'cello once before the King of Prussia with such effect that the king said he'd never heard anything like it before. The town was naturally very proud of the trio, and particularly of Dr. Teutonstring, who, though far from being a muscular man, had once played the bass-viol for sixteen consecutive hours in the musical contest at the Schnitzelhammerstein carnival, beating by one hour and twenty-two minutes the strongest and most enduring bass-viol player in Germany. They were the most amiable old gentlemen in the world. It very seldom happened that they failed to agree, which was rather wonderful, because it often happens, unhappily, that musicians grow jealous of one another, and say and do things that make it impossible for them to live together peaceably. You may not all of you remember that famous and very sad instance of the lengths to which this jealousy is sometimes allowed to run wherein Luigi Sparragini, the well-known Italian violinist, in his rage at the applause received at a concert by his rival, Siegfried von Heimstetter, broke a Stradivarius violin valued at a thousand pounds over Von Heimstetter's head, to be rebuked in return by Von Heimstetter, who induced Sparragini to look at the mechanism of a grand piano he had, letting the cover fall on the other's head as soon as he had poked it in, thereby utterly ruining the piano and severely injuring Sparragini's nose.

Nothing of this kind, as I have intimated, ever marred the serenity of the three amiable musicians of Schnitzelhammerstein-on-the-Zugvitz.

"We have no cause each other to be jealous of," Herr von Kärlingtongs had said. "I the fiddle play; they the fiddle do not play."

"True," observed Heinrich Flatz. "The potato just as well the watermelon might be jealous of. If I the fiddle played, then might I Von Kärlingtongs be jealous of. Therefore also already can the same be said regarding Teutonstring. In no manner are we each other the rivals of."

In all of which, as Hans Pumpernickel said to me, there was much common-sense. "Discord is not music," said he, "and if these men were discordant they would not be musicians. If they were not musicians they would have to make a living in some other kind of business. They are not fit for any other kind of business, wherefore they are wise as well as amiable."

The consequence of all this harmony between the three dear old gentlemen was that they were always together. They practised together, and on public occasions they played together, and their fellow-townsmen were delighted with them. At weddings they played the wedding-marches, each as earnestly as though he were play-

ing a solo. At the Mayor's banquets they
were always present, adding much to the
pleasure of these sumptuous repasts by
the soft and beautiful strains which they
discoursed. "I am not a king," said
Mayor Ehrenbreitstein upon one of these
occasions; "but if I were, I could not hear
better music. We have an orchestra without a court. What more can we desire?"

"Nothing," said Hans Pumpernickel,
"unless it be another tune."

"A good idea," cried one of the aldermen.
"Let us have another tune."

And so the cry would go about the board,
and the three happy old gentlemen would
good-naturedly go to work again and play
another tune. It came about very naturally, then, that whenever a rival band of
musicians, desirous of wresting the laurels
from the respective brows of Herren Von
Kärlingtongs, Teutonstring, and Flatz,
came to Schnitzelhammerstein, they found
them so strongly intrenched in the affections
of the people that, while they lived and
played in harmony together, no others could
hope to make a living from music in that
community. They rapidly grew rich; for it

178

came to pass that, with the exception of house
rent, and new strings for their instruments,
and other mere incidentals of a musician's
work, they had no expenses to pay. Their
food cost them nothing, they attended so
many banquets; and when, occasionally,
a day would come upon which no break-
fast, luncheon, or dinner required their
services, it was always found that they
had carried away enough fruit and cake
and other dainties from the affairs that
had been given to last them through such
rare intervals as found them without an
engagement.

In other respects, too, did these worthies
show themselves entitled to be called wise.
Some five years after they began to grow
famous in Schnitzelhammerstein - on - the-
Zugvitz some of their admirers suggested
that they ought not to confine themselves
to the small town in which they had waxed
so great, but should go out into the world
and dazzle all mankind by the brilliance of
their playing.

"The great orchestras of Austria," said
one of these, "do not content themselves
with laurels won at home. They travel

into far countries, and win fame and fortune all the world over. Why do not you go?"

"We will talk it over," Herr Teutonstring replied. "I for one am opposed to making such a trip, because I am an old man, and my bass-viol is heavy."

"Can you not send it about by freight?" said the man who proposed the scheme.

"Would you send your child by freight?" asked Herr Teutonstring.

"I would not," returned the other.

"No more can I send my bass-viol by freight," said Herr Teutonstring, fondly twanging the strings of his huge instrument. "This is my whole family. I love it as I would a child for whom I must care; as a father who has helped me to become what I am. Nevertheless, we will talk it over."

And they did talk it over, and as a result decided that the world, if it desired to hear them play, must come to Schnitzelhammerstein-on-the-Zugvitz.

"If we go," said Herr Von Kärlingtongs, "who will provide music for Schnitzelhammerstein-on-the-Zugvitz?"

"Who, indeed?" said Heinrich Flatz, gazing at the floor after the manner of the truly wise man.

"Since you have both asked that question," said Herr Teutonstring, "out of mere politeness I must answer it. My answer is, briefly, I haven't the slightest idea."

"But some one must," persisted Von Kärlingtongs.

"Yes," said the others.

"Then one of two things must happen," said Von Kärlingtongs. "Either by our absence the people of this town must be deprived of good music, which would be very ungrateful of us, who have gained so much profit from them, or they must discover that there are others who can play as well as we do, whereby we would cease to be the greatest in the world—which strikes me as bad policy."

"Von Kärlingtongs," said Heinrich Flatz, with tears of joy in his eyes, "you are not only a musician, you are a thinker."

"Do not flatter me, my dear Flatz," said Von Kärlingtongs, modestly. "You do not know what a struggle it is to me to keep from giving way to pride."

"Over the Plum-Pudding"

"Well, I agree to all that you have said," said Herr Teutonstring; "and I have to add that, as we are only young in spirit, and as my bass-viol is very heavy, I think we should be content to remain at home."

"Particularly," added Heinrich Flatz, "in view of the fact that there can be but one result. We should succeed. Now where is the gratification in success? Simply in the knowledge that you have succeeded. We know that now. Wherefore why should we put ourselves to inconveniences simply to find out what we already know? Does a man with a pantryful of tarts go seeking tarts? He does not—"

"If he is wise," said Herr Teutonstring.

"And we are wise," added Herr von Kärlingtongs.

"Which settles the point. We'll stay at home," said Herr Flatz.

And they did, and subsequent events showed the wisdom of their course, for in less than a year's time the King came to Schnitzelhammerstein-on-the-Zugvitz.

Some said that he stopped there merely because there was a better luncheon-counter at the railway station than anywhere else along the road. Others persisted that his Majesty had heard of the marvellous powers of the three musicians, and, being fond of music, had travelled all the way from the capital, a distance of more than a hundred miles, to hear them. However this was, the fact remained that the King announced that for two hours he would be the guest of the little city concerning which we have spoken so much. The town naturally was all of a flutter, and great preparations were made to receive his Majesty.

"I will make a speech," said the Mayor, "and our orchestra can serenade his Majesty."

"The serenade is a good idea," said Hans Pumpernickel, innocently. "Shall I inform Herr Teutonstring and his fellow-players that that is your opinion?"

"As a rule, I avoid having opinions," said the Mayor, "but in this instance I think it is safe to hazard one. You may inform the gentlemen."

"And the speech?" suggested Hans.

"We'll see about that," said the Mayor. "If I can get a good one, I shall deliver it."

"Very well," said Hans. "I'll try to

think of something for you to say. Meanwhile I'll see Von Kärlingtongs."

Hans did as he said, and, despite their wisdom, the three musicians were as much in a flutter as the rest of the city. To play before the King was an unexpected honor, although Heinrich Flatz affected to treat it as quite an ordinary thing.

"He is a very fair judge of music," said Flatz, patronizingly, "for a King. I think that, after all, we'd better do our best."

"Yes," said Von Kärlingtongs, "you are right, as usual, though I will say right here that, in doing my best, I am actuated as much by my loyalty to my art as by any other motive. I *always* do my best."

"And I also," put in Teutonstring. "Now the question that arises is what *is* our best?"

"That *is* indeed the question," said Herr Flatz. "I, having already had the honor to play before his Majesty, am perhaps better fitted than either of you to say what he likes. When I was so distinguished I played Djorski's Symphony in B Minor. Therefore I contend that that is what we should play. His Majesty remarked that he had never heard anything like it before. He would doubtless like to hear it again. Therefore I say that is the thing for us to play."

"Ordinarily," said Teutonstring, "I can agree with Herr Flatz, but this time I cannot. *I* am at my best in Darmstadter's Oratorio. There can be no question about it that the bass-viol is at its highest, most ennobling point in that composition, which is why I say let us have the Oratorio. The King, having heard the Symphony in B Minor, would naturally rather hear something else. The Symphony, no doubt, would awaken pleasant memories, but the Oratorio would give him something new to remember in the future."

"There is much in what you say, Herr Teutonstring," put in Von Kärlingtongs. "There is also much in what my dear friend Flatz says; but it seems to me that there is more in what I have to say than in the combined suggestions of both of you. The Symphony in B Minor is excellent, the Oratorio is quite as excellent, but neither of them comes up to Dboriak's Moonlight Sonata, which, when I play it, makes me

"Over the Plum-Pudding"

feel as though the whole world lay at my feet—as if I were the King of all creation. Now I am a man; the King is a man; we are both men. It is but natural to suppose that if this Sonata makes me, a man, feel like the King of all creation, it will also make that other man, the King, feel the same way. What is our object in playing before the King? To please him. How can we best please him? Simply by making him feel that he is the King of all creation. Perfectly simple, my dear Flatz. Plain as a pikestaff, Teutonstring. Therefore let us play Dboriak's Moonlight Sonata."

It was thus that the three musicians, who had always hitherto agreed, came to have the first difference of their lives, and what made it seem worse than all was that this difference occurred at a time which seemed to them in their secret hearts to be the greatest event of their lives. Perhaps it was the very importance of this event that made each of them firm in his belief that he was right and the others wrong. Neither would yield to the others, and an hour before the arrival of the royal train found Flatz

A Great Composer

determined to play the Symphony, Teutonstring determined to play the Oratorio, and
Von Kärlingtongs equally immovable in
his determination to play the Moonlight
Sonata, and nothing else. They labored
with one another in vain. Doctor Teutonstring tried to win over Herr Flatz, saying
that if together they should play the Oratorio
they could let Von Kärlingtongs render
the Sonata without much harm, since the
bass-viol and 'cello together could drown the
sounds of the violin. Herr Flatz would
agree to a combination of two against one
only in case the Symphony were selected,
and when the King arrived no change whatsoever had been made in the determination
of the musicians. Ruin stared them in the
face, but each preferred ruin to a base sur-
render of what he thought to be for the
best.

Of course, as the King alighted from the
train the people cheered, and, when the
Mayor rose to greet him with the speech
he had to make, they cheered again, but
these cheers were as nothing to those which
greeted the appearance of the musicians.
Many nations had kings; all cities had

mayors; what city had such an orchestra?
No wonder they cheered.

And then the serenade began.

Herr Flatz resined his bow and began
the Symphony in B Minor, while Von
Kärlingtongs and Teutonstring, equally
determined, started in on the opening meas-
ures of the Sonata and Oratorio respec-
tively.

"It's something new they've got up for
the occasion," whispered the people, as the
three men fiddled away with all their
strength.

"A most original composition!" said the
King to the Chancellor.

"I never heard such discord in my life,"
said a small boy on the outskirts of the
crowd.

Still they kept on. The Symphony and
the Oratorio were longer than the Sonata,
so that Von Kärlingtongs soon found himself outdone by his fellow-players, but,
nothing daunted, he played the Sonata over
again. And so it went, until, with a final
grand burst of notes (I was almost about
to say harmony), they stopped.

"Magnificent!" said the King.

"THE THREE FIDDLED WITH ALL THEIR STRENGTH"

A Great Composer

"A really classic composition," murmured the Chancellor.

And the people shrieked with delight.

The musicians, perspiring with excitement, stood overcome with surprise. They had succeeded beyond their wildest hopes, but the King brought them to their senses in a minute by asking:

"What is the composer's name?"

"What 'll we tell him?" moaned Teutonstring. "It will never do to confess what we have done now."

"I'm sure I don't know," returned Flatz, with a shiver.

"The composer's name, sir," replied Von Kärlingtongs, more ready of wit than the others—"the composer's name is—ah—is—"

"Well?" said the King, impatiently.

"It is Kärlingteutonflatz," said Von Kärlingtongs.

"Give him a thousand marks," said the King, "and distribute a thousand more to these gentlemen," he added.

And then the royal party proceeded on its way.

As for the composer, Kärlingteutonflatz,

he was never heard of again; but several other eminent musicians modelled their music after his, and obtained a renown that was not only world-wide, but has lasted until this day.

The three musicians of Schnitzelhammerstein-on-the-Zugvitz, when they had recovered from their surprise and excitement, began to smile, and never stopped until they died—and I am not certain that they stopped then—nor did they ever confide their secret to any one but Hans Pumpernickel, who in turn confided it to me, so that this is really the first time the public has been let into the secret origin of what was then the music of the future and what is to-day the music of the present.

How Fritz Became a Wizard

How Fritz Became a Wizard

T was a lovely summer afternoon at Schnitzelhammerstein-on-the-Zugvitz, and Hans Pumpernickel and I, having little else to do, idled along the sylvan path that for five or six miles follows the winding course of the famous little river. Hans was in a very talkative mood that day. He had quite recently been re-elected Mayor of the town in which he lived, after a hard campaign of six weeks, during which time he had not been allowed to say anything, for fear of spoiling his chances of re-election.

"And now that it is over, and I am safely in office once more, I am going to make up for lost time," he said. "Having kept silent for six weeks, I shall now talk three times as much as usual for three. I am fat with suppressed conversation, and I must get rid of it, or I shall burst."

"Over the Plum-Pudding"

So, as I have told you, he was very talkative, and on that afternoon he told me enough stories to fill an encyclopædia, most of which, I regret to say, I have forgotten, but some of which, also, I remember perfectly. The one telling how Fritz von Hatzfeldt became a wizard was one of these latter, and it seemed to me quite good enough to tell to you. It came about in this way. When nearing the point where the celebrated Baron Laubenheimer, at the risk of his life, once plunged into the Zugvitz to rescue Johanna Johannisberg from drowning—a heroic act, the story of which I hope some day to tell you—we perceived walking ahead of us a strange-looking old gentleman, clad in a long, flowing robe with a border embroidered with mystic figures. He wore spectacles—or, rather, the rims of spectacles, without glass; for, as I learned afterwards, though his eyes were in good condition, his ideas as to the dignity of his profession compelled him to appear as wise as possible, and he had discovered that nothing imparts to the face of man so much of the appearance of wisdom as spectacles.

How Fritz Became a Wizard

"That," said Hans Pumpernickel, in response to my question, "is our town wizard, Fritz von Hatzfeldt, and I may add that the town has never had a better one. When I was running for Mayor this last time against Pflueger, who, as you may remember, was the opposing candidate, Von Hatzfeldt was consulted by my friends as to my chances; for, as town wizard, it is his duty to prophesy. His answer was wonderfully quick, and absolutely accurate. 'Who will be elected,' said he, 'Pumpernickel or Pflueger?' 'Yes,' said they, 'that is the question.' 'I will consult the stars,' said Von Hatzfeldt, withdrawing to his observatory. Now, his predecessor, Rosenstein, would have taken a week to return his verdict, but Von Hatzfeldt's strong point is quickness. He remained with the stars no longer than two hours, and then, emerging from his observatory, he said, 'I have consulted, and the heavens tell me that the name of our next Mayor will begin with the letter P.' And it was so. Pumpernickel was elected, and Pflueger was defeated. Was not that an extraordinary, even a wonderful prophecy?"

"Over the Plum-Pudding"

"Very," I assented. "That man must be a genius; I should like to meet him."

"I think it can be arranged," said Hans. "I will ask him if you may." And he hurried on to overtake the wizard. In a moment he returned.

"Well," I said, "does he consent to my meeting him?"

"Yes," said Hans. "Only, with his customary wisdom, he says that, to meet him, you should be coming towards him from in front. He says that people can only be said to meet when face to face. 'You do not meet the man who walks behind you, Mr. Mayor,' he said; 'but if your friend will take a short-cut through the woods to the old rock two hundred paces on, he can then approach me from before, and then we shall meet.'"

"That suits me," said I, and, making the cut through the woods, I reached the rock, turned back, and soon stood face to face with the wizard. "I am glad to know you," said I, as Pumpernickel introduced us.

"I was about to make a similar remark myself," returned Von Hatzfeldt, "but concluded not to, and for this reason: to tell you that would be to tell you something you already knew. If I had not been glad to meet you, I could have turned aside and avoided the meeting. Now, my notion of the duties of a professional wizard is that he should tell people only those things which they do not know, and should avoid wasting his breath in imparting useless information."

"A very sage observation," said Pumpernickel.

"And what else did you expect?" queried the wizard, gazing through his unglazed spectacles upon the Mayor. "Mark you, Mr. Mayor, it is the business of wizards to make sage observations. You might as well try to purchase a diamond necklace of a green-grocer as look for unwise remarks from a professional wizard."

"I'll test his powers of prophecy now," said Hans to me, in a whisper.

"Do," I replied. "I shall be delighted, for I never met a real prophet before."

"Ah, Herr Wizard," said Hans, addressing Von Hatzfeldt, "what do you think about the weather?"

"Over the Plum-Pudding"

"It is very fair—now," replied the wizard.

"Now, eh?" said Hans. "Then you think it will not always be so?"

"No," replied the wizard, glancing up into the heavens. "No. To you there is nothing in the skies to foretell a change, but to me there is much. Before the winter is over, Hans Pumpernickel, we shall have snow. I read it in the stars."

"Stars?" I cried. "By day?"

"And why not?" returned the wizard. "Do you think because you do not see them that therefore the stars are all destroyed?"

To this I had no answer, and before I could recover myself Fritz von Hatzfeldt had passed on.

"Isn't he a wonder?" said Pumpernickel.

"He is more than a wonder," I replied. "He is a four-hundred-and-tender"—a joke, by the way, which Hans Pumpernickel did not appreciate.

"Whence do your wizards come?" I asked.

"There is no rule," Pumpernickel answered. "The wisest person in town is generally selected, though, as for Fritz, he studied wizardry under Rosenstein. It was curious the way it happened. Fritz was the son

How Fritz Became a Wizard

of a farmer, who sent him to school when he was very young, and at the age of five he could read so well that he couldn't be got to leave his books and help gather in the crops. At seven his father, in a fit of anger at what he termed the boy's laziness, turned him out of doors, and Fritz came to Schnitzel-hammerstein to seek his fortune. The first position he held was as boy in a butcher-shop, but he had to give that up, because, having gone for weeks without sufficient food, his appetite was a serious menace to the butcher's stock, which the butcher did not discover until Fritz had eaten one whole side of beef. Then he became candy-puller for a molasses-candy-maker, who employed him without counting upon his sweet tooth. This he was compelled to give up after having consumed two weeks' salary's worth of candy in two days. It was this second rebuff that brought him to Rosenstein's notice. While standing in his laboratory one morning the wizard heard a piping little voice cry out, 'Excuse me, sir, but don't you want an assistant?'

"'An assistant what?' asked Rosenstein.

"'An assistant whatever you are,' return-

ed the owner of the little voice, who was
none other than Fritz.

"The answer pleased Rosenstein. He recognized wisdom in it; for that it was wise
no one will deny.

"'Don't you know what I am?' he asked.

"'Yes,' said Fritz. 'You are a very nice
old gentleman.'

"Rosenstein laughed. 'True,' he said.
'But I am also the town wizard.'

"'Then will I be the assistant town
wizard,' said Fritz. 'What do wizards do
—whiz?'

"'I'll take you in for a week and let you
see,' said Rosenstein, and little Fritz was
employed to do errands. But alas for him!
The wizard, though he liked him much,
could not afford to keep him. He had not
counted upon Fritz's appetite any more than
the butcher had, and again was the boy
sent forth. This time, however, he was
sent forth in a kindly way. 'You are a
good boy, Fritz, and I like you, and I think
you would make a good wizard some day,
for you have a wise way about you for your
years, but I am too poor to feed you. I will
say to you, however, that if you ever make

"'YOU ARE A VERY NICE OLD GENTLEMAN'"

How Fritz Became a Wizard

your fortune in this world, then will I be
glad to receive you back again and point
out to you the path you should pursue if
you would some day succeed me in my
office. Make your fortune first, my boy,
then come to me.'

"' Can't I stay if I lose my appetite?' asked
Fritz, mournfully.

"' Ah, but you mustn't do that,' the wizard
answered. 'An appetite is a splendid thing
—a fortune in itself—but you must also
have another fortune in itself to maintain
it. Go, my boy, and bless you!'

"Poor Fritz! This last failure discour-
aged him wofully. He had no money, no
home, nobody to go to. His condition was
a dreadful one; but the Fates had a happy life in store for him. He wandered out
along this very path up to the big rock, and
sat down to meditate, and as he meditated
he observed, as the tide of the river went
down, it uncovered the entrance to what
appeared to be a huge cavern. 'Humph!'
said Fritz. 'Looks like a cave. Maybe I
can use that for a place to live in. There
may be one or two dry spots inside where I
could sleep, and I could always come out

at low tide if I wanted to. There's house rent saved, anyhow.'

"Speaking thus, he climbed down into the cavern, and, as he had hoped, found plenty of dry places, and from that time on it became his home. He occasionally made a few marks by doing chores for people around about Schnitzelhammerstein, and with them he supplied himself with food and furniture. The spring-time came, and with it a freshet which completely covered up the entrance to the cavern night and day, high tide or low, and Fritz found himself shut up in his strange home for two whole dreary months. Escape was impossible. The sole sustenance he had was an occasional fish he caught in some of the pools.

"It was not until he had been in this cavernous prison for five weeks that he noticed a most unique thing about it. *Night and day it was always brilliantly lighted!* On the Monday night of the fifth week this singular fact flashed upon the boy's mind. How was it? Whence could the light come? It was not sunlight, because that would not shine by night. What, then, was the secret of the light in the cave? The

"THE LITTLE FELLOW MUSED OFT AND LONG THEREON"

little fellow mused oft and long thereon, and finally he reached a conclusion, which, like all his conclusions, was a wise one.

"'This is worth investigating. I will investigate,' he cried. 'Meditation is good in its way, but if a thing is past mental comprehension, then investigation of an active sort is in order. In the first place, the light does not come from above; it streams in through that chink in the rock off to the left. I will slide through that chink and see what is to be seen.'

"In an instant he had done so, and— there lay his fortune. Lying upon the soft earth floor of the adjoining cave was a diamond, dazzling in its lustre, and large as a hen's egg. So brilliant was it that all about it was lighted up as though by electricity. In a second Fritz pounced upon it and held it aloft. It nearly blinded him, but he held on to it like grim death. It was his, and only his. His fortune was made.

"Three weeks later the waters subsided, and Fritz went forth into the world with his diamond."

"But," said I, "a diamond like that would

be very hard to sell, and people might not understand how it had come into the possession of a small boy who had always been poor."

"True," said Pumpernickel, "and Fritz thought of that. 'Too sudden riches fly suddenly away,' he observed. 'I will proceed slowly.' *He didn't show that diamond to any one until he had made his fortune.*"

"Then how—how did he make his fortune?" I asked.

"He sold its light," said Hans. "It does not sound probable, but it is true. In those days we had no gas or electricity to light our public squares or ballrooms or libraries, and Fritz, noting this, bought a small lantern with ground-glass sides, so that the diamond could shed its light without itself being seen, and, putting his diamond into it, rented it out for public meetings, for ballroom illumination—in fact, to any who stood in need of a strong, powerful light. Scientists from all Germany flocked in to see it, and besought him to divulge the secret of the light, but he would not until he had accumulated a fortune, and then he let the world into his confidence. Meanwhile he

"IT NEARLY BLINDED HIM"

had gone back to Rosenstein, and had learned the art of being a wizard, and when Rosenstein died he was unanimously called to fill the vacancy."

"And what became of the diamond?"

"That," said Hans, "is a mystery. Some say that Von Hatzfeldt has it yet, but burglars who have searched his house high and low a thousand times say that he hasn't it."

"And he—what does he say?"

"He declines to speak of it," said Hans, simply.

"Well," said I, "that is a very remarkable tale."

"Yes," said Hans, "but then Fritz von Hatzfeldt is a very remarkable wizard, for how a man can be as wise as he and know so little passes all comprehension."

Rise and Fall of the Poet Gregory

Rise and Fall of the Poet Gregory

ONE night after dining with Hans Pumpernickel at his house in Schnitzelhammerstein - on - the - Zugvitz, I recalled to his mind that he had promised some time to introduce me to the three sages of the town—the only persons residing there who at all approached Fritz von Hatzfeldt, the wizard, in wisdom.

"True," said he, "I did promise that, and if you like I will take you to them this evening. They are a wonderful trio, and between you and me, I really think they know more in a day than Von Hatzfeldt does in a year. The maxims of Otto the Shoemaker alone contain wisdom enough to set ten wizards up in business. Did you ever hear any of Otto the Shoemaker's maxims?"

"Over the Plum-Pudding"

"No," said I. "I never even heard of Otto the Shoemaker. Does he write maxims?"

"Not exactly," replied Hans, filling his pipe and putting on his hat. "He cannot write, but he can speak. He says maxims."

"How interesting!" I observed, following Hans's example and putting on my hat and filling my pipe also. "I should like to hear some of them."

"You shall," replied Hans. "Here is one of them: 'One never misses one's shoes until he has to do without them.' That, you see, is undeniable, and is full of wisdom. Then there was this one addressed to his son: 'Rise in the world, but be careful how. The man who goes up in a balloon cannot stay up after the gas gives out. Therefore, my son, rise not up at random, even as the balloonist does, but rather move up slowly but surely, like him who builds a tower of rock beneath him, and is thus able to stay up as long as he pleases.'"

"Wonderful," said I. "And you say that this philosopher, this deep thinker, this Maximilian, is content to remain a shoemaker?"

Rise and Fall of the Poet Gregory

"Yes," Hans answered, "he is, for, as he himself once said, 'The throne itself rests upon society merely, but upon what does society stand? Boots and shoes! I make boots and shoes, wherefore I am the cornerstone of the empire.'"

"I must meet this Otto the Shoemaker," was my response, and to that end Hans Pumpernickel and I went out to the little back street where Otto the Shoemaker, Eisenberg the Keysmith, and Jurgurson the Innkeeper, the three sages of the town, dwelt peacefully and happily together in neighborly intercourse. We found them having a quiet little gossip after tea. Eisenberg was leaning out of his shop window, his long, white clay pipe unfilled in his hand, lovingly discoursing to Otto the Shoemaker, who, clad in his leather apron, hung upon his every word as though each were a pearl of thought, and to Jurgurson the Innkeeper, who sat opposite him with a look upon his face which indicated how much he marvelled at the wisdom which bubbled out of Eisenberg's lips like water from a geyser.

"It is as I tell you," Eisenberg was saying; "thought is the key to every mystery; wherefore I, being the maker of keys of all sorts, necessarily manufacture thoughts. It is a part of my business. Why, therefore, should the world express surprise at my being a thinker?"

"Wherefore, indeed?" replied Jurgurson; "or me, too? As the keeper of the inn is it not for me to dispense entertainment for man and beast? Is not wisdom the entertainment of many men, and do not many men come here? Why should I, too, then, not have wisdom on draught just as likewise I have ginger-ale and lemonade?"

"You are both right," put in Otto the Shoemaker. "And as for me, what? This: the labor of the shoemaker is confining. I am kept at my bench all day. I must have exercise or I die; with my body busy at my trade, what can I exercise else? My wits—yah! That is, then, the cause of no surprise that I, too, am sagacious."

"We have never said anything more wise," said Eisenberg, proudly, and the others agreed with him.

At this point Hans presented me to the sages.

Rise and Fall of the Poet Gregory

"Gentlemen," he said, after he had given to each an appropriate greeting, "I have brought with me one who wishes to know you. He is an American and a poet."

"Ach!" cried Eisenberg. "An American — that is good. A poet? Well we shall see. That is not always so good. Do you write, sir?"

"Occasionally," I answered.

"Good," said Otto. "That is better than often."

"True," assented Jurgurson, "though not so good as hardly ever."

I laughed. "You do not seem to think much of poets," said I.

"We do not say that," said Otto. "We do not know you as a poet, and so we do not pass judgment. When one says because one or two, or even two thousand, shoemakers are bad, all shoemakers are bad, one speaks foolishness. So with the poets. Because Heinrich von Scribbhausen writes bad stuff, you do not therefore write bad stuff. A poet should be judged, not by his shoes, but by his poems. I, a shoemaker, must not be judged by my poems, but by my shoes, which points a moral, and that moral is, what is sauce for the goose is not always sauce for the gander. The gander may be a person who makes fine clothes. The goose should not be judged by his clothes, but the gander should; therefore, never judge a man for what he ain't."

"Bravo!" cried Jurgurson. "I could not have spoken more wisely myself."

"Nor I," said Eisenberg. "Yet I could add somewhat. You do not print your poems?"

"Of course," I replied, "and why not?"

"It is a great risk," sighed Eisenberg. "Particularly for poets, for, as Otto has well said, the world cannot judge a man for what he is not; so if a shoemaker print a bad book of poems, there is no risk. The poems will be judged as the work of a shoemaker, and, though bad, may still be good for a shoemaker to have written; but for a poet to print bad poems, that is as risky as for a shoemaker to make bad shoes."

At this point my guide, Hans Pumpernickel, feeling perhaps that the conversation was not exactly pleasant for me, in spite of the undoubted wisdom of the sages' remarks, handed his tobacco-pouch to the keysmith, having observed that Eisenberg's pipe was empty.

"Thank you, no," said Eisenberg, handing it back, "I do not smoke tobacco. It is tobacco which makes of smoking an injurious pastime. To me the pleasure of smoking is the caressing of a pipe, the holding of it in one's hands, the occasional putting of it into one's mouth and puffing. Therefore I keep my pipe to caress, to hold, to put into my mouth, and to puff upon. The tobacco, which does not agree with me, I never use."

Otto and Jurgurson beamed proudly upon their fellow-sage. It was evident that in him they recognized the centre of all wisdom.

"But as for poets," said Eisenberg, turning to me, "I should like to tell you about Gregory—the poet Gregory. Did you ever hear of him?"

"No," said I.

"Ah! See then!" cried Eisenberg. "It proves my point. He is unknown already, and all for why? Because his poems were printed, for until they were printed they were not unknown."

"Magnificently put!" cried the shoemaker.

"Logical as logic itself!" said the innkeeper.

"And what is the story of Gregory?" I asked, interested hugely and almost as enthusiastic over the whimsical wisdom of the keysmith as his fellow-wiseacres.

"Gregory," said Eisenberg, "was the first name. His last name I shall not give you for two reasons. The first reason is that, if I gave it to you, I should betray a confidence reposed in me by his family. The second reason is that I have forgotten it. That is the sad part of it all. When a name begins to be forgotten by one, or even two persons, its trip to oblivion is rapid. Even I, who used to worship him as a poet, have forgotten the name he made for himself."

The keysmith sighed sorrowfully as he spoke, and I began to believe with him, though without knowing the reason therefor, that Gregory's cause was indeed a lost one. There was silence for a full minute, during which Eisenberg puffed thoughtfully upon his empty pipe, blowing imaginary clouds of smoke out into the air, and then he spoke.

"Gregory was not of high birth, but early in life his parents saw that he was not destined to follow successfully the career of a peasant. He was of an inquiring mind. He was not content to know that grass was green and water wet. He wished to know why grass was green and water wet, and when, in response to questions of this nature, his father, a practical person, would send him out to the stables to milk the cows, or to the grindstone to sharpen the scythe, Gregory's soul revolted within him. 'You will never make a peasant,' said his father. 'Not a peasant of the fields,' the boy replied, 'but a peasant of learning, perhaps. I would not mind milking the cow of knowledge, and filling the pail of my mind with lactated information; nor should I mind sharpening my wits upon the grindstone of thought.' And at these words his father would stare at him and say that one who had such command of mysterious language did not need Greek to conceal his thoughts from his hearers; and he would add an invitation, which Gregory perforce always accepted, to retire to the fagot-room with him and receive corporal punishment at his hands. So it went for several years, during which Gregory read everything that came within reach, until finally one morning he said to his father: "Why do you persist in making a peasant of me when I wish to be a poet? What is the odds to you? Nay, more, father, do not the words peasant and poet both begin with a P and end with a T? What difference can it make if the ends be the same?'—which so enraged his father that Gregory was disowned by him, and another boy adopted in his place.

"Then Gregory came here to Schnitzelhammerstein - on - the - Zugvitz, and at a time when Rudolf von Pepperpotz, the solemn Baron of Humpfelhimmel, happened to stand in need of a secretary and librarian. How it came about that Gregory was so unfortunate as to obtain the position is neither here nor there. Suffice it to say that he became the secretary and librarian of the Baron, and from that time on he was happy. He lived among books, and while at times he found his duties arduous, he was

nevertheless content, for he was a philosopher."

"I'd rather be content than eat," said the
innkeeper.

"Indeed, yes," said Otto, "for entertainment is better than dyspepsia, and poor
eating comes more of the one than the other."

"By careful economy," continued Eisenberg, "Gregory soon managed to amass
a little fortune, and then he felt he might
safely venture to write a little himself, and he
did so. He wrote poems about the moon,
odes to commonplace things, like scissors
and dust-pans, but he was wise enough
not to publish any of his verse. Then he
married, and occasionally he would recite
his verses to his wife, who said they were
magnificent. She in turn repeated them
to her friends, and they said, as she had,
that they were unsurpassed. Still Gregory
would not print them, though it soon got
noised about that he was a great poet. And
so it went. Finally, finding himself sub-
jected to great temptation to print his writings, he put everything he had written into a
casket, and, having a small closet construct-
ed in the walls of his house, he placed the

"Over the Plum-Pudding"

casket in that closet, locked the iron door upon it and threw away the key. Time went on, and people daily, their curiosity excited, talked more and more of Gregory's poetry; they even sent delegations to him, requesting him to have his rhymes printed, but he was faithful to his resolution, and when he died he was looked upon as a great writer, without having printed a line. Time passed and his reputation grew. Three generations passed by. His children and their children and their children's children came, lived, and died, and constantly his fame increased, and people said, 'Ah, yes; so and so is a great poet, but the poems of Gregory! You should have heard them. They were sublime.'

"But two years ago there came an unhappy day. Some one laughed at the mention of Gregory's name and cast doubt upon the tradition that he had written, and his great-grandson, foolishly, I thought, and recklessly, as has since been proved, offered to prove the truth of the tradition by opening the closet which for a century had remained closed, and publishing the writings of his ancestor. I was sent for as

keysmith to open the door, and when it was
opened there stood the casket, and in the
casket were found the poems.

"'Let that suffice,' said I to his great-
grandson. 'You have proved your point.'

"'I will prove it to the world,' said he.
'I will publish the poems.'"

Here Eisenberg sighed.

"He did so," he resumed mournfully,
"and another idol was shattered. The
poems were the worst you ever read, and
from that time on the name of Gregory the
poet began to sink into oblivion, where it
now lies. Had his descendants been less
weak, his name would still have remained a
household word, such is the force of tradition.
As it is, the printed volume is the best tes-
timony that the great poet Gregory was nothing but a commonplace rhymester whose
name was not worthy of remembrance.

"And that, sir," concluded Eisenberg,
bowing politely to me, "is why I say that a
poet who does not publish runs less risk of
failing as a poet than he who does publish."

And I? Well, how could I deny that
Eisenberg was right? He had proved his
point only too well, and even that night,

"Over the Plum-Pudding"

on my return home, I went to my little portfolio and utterly destroyed the dozen or more poems I had written that day. If you will take my word for it, you will think them greater than you might if you insisted upon reading them.

"What think you?" asked Hans, as we went home? "Are they not wise?"

"Wiser than the Three Men of Gotham who went to sea in a bowl," said I, "for I do not believe that Otto, Eisenberg, or Jurgurson would go to sea at all."

"True," was Hans's comment, "for as Otto well says in one of his maxims, 'For a sailor with his sea-legs on there is nothing like the sea, but for a shoemaker who lives by shoes alone, dry land is by much the solider foundation.'"

The Loss of the "Gretchen B."

The Loss of the "Gretchen B."

A TALE OF A PIRATE GHOST, FOUND FLOATING IN A WATER-BOTTLE.

I

THE DISCOVERY

T was a very pleasant evening in July. Hans Pumpernickel, who had just laid down the duties of Mayor of Schnitzelhammerstein - on - the - Zugvitz, after having filled that lofty office for eight years, was walking with me along the river-front at its busiest point.

"Let us go out on the wharf," said Hans, as we neared its entrance. "When I was a small boy I used to take pleasure in sitting upon the twine-piece of the wharf and letting my legs dingle over."

I scratched my head for a moment before I saw exactly what he meant by "twine-piece" and "dingle."

"Over the Plum-Pudding"

"You speak English very well, **Pum**pernickel," said I; "but what you should have said was 'string-piece' and '**dangle**,' not 'twine-piece' and 'dingle.'"

"But," he protested, "is not a piece of twine a piece of string?"

"Yes," I replied; "but—"

"Then why may not a 'twine-piece' be a 'string-piece'? And as for 'dingle,' is it not the present tense of the verb 'to dingle'? Dingle, dangle, dungle—like sing, sang, sung? You would not say 'letting him sang' — it would be 'letting him sing'; wherefore, why not say 'letting my legs dingle over,' and avoid saying 'letting my legs dangle over'?"

"Oh, well, have it your own way," said I; and, having reached the end of the wharf, we sat down there, and shortly found our legs "dingling" over the water in the most approved style.

"It is a hard sort of a seat," said I, after a moment or two of silence, as we gazed upon the river flowing by.

"True," said Hans, philosophically, "though it is not made of hard wood. Let us take a boat and have a row."

The Loss of the "Gretchen B."

I agreed, and we hired a small skiff and paddled idly down the stream. We had not gone far when the bow of our craft bumped up against something which scraped against the side of the boat as we passed.

"What was that?" said Pumpernickel.

"I don't know," said I, indifferently. "Nothing, I guess."

"What nonsense you talk sometimes!" he retorted. "It must have been something. We'll retreat and see."

Suiting the action to the words, Hans backed water with his oars, and in the dim light of the moon we soon descried the object of our search—a curious old earthen vessel floating in the river, bobbing up and down very much like a buoy. It looked like a water-bottle of two centuries ago, and, indeed, upon investigation turned out to be such.

"Aha!" cried Hans, triumphantly, as I lifted the bottle into the boat, "it *was* something, after all. I knew it could not be nothing. Is it empty of contents?"

I turned the vessel bottom side up, and nothing came out of it, but there was a distinct thud within which betrayed the presence of some solid substance.

"It is not empty of contents," said I, giving it another shake, "but it hasn't any table to show what those contents are."

"Oh, we don't need a table," said Hans, failing to appreciate the subtle humor of my remark. "Just shake it out."

With a sigh over my lost joke, I did as I was bidden, and soon, after a vigorous shaking and the removal of a cork which I had not previously noticed, the substance within issued forth through the bottle's neck.

"Dear me," said I. "It appears to be manuscript."

"Let me see," said Hans. "Ah," he observed, "it is writing. Why did you say it was manuscript?"

"That is writing," I explained.

"That may be," said he, "but why waste your tongue on three syllables when two will do?"

I ignored the question and put another.

"Can you read it?" I asked.

"With difficulty," he said, "by this light.

228

The Loss of the "Gretchen B."

Let us return to my rooms and see if we can decimate it."

"Decipher, decipher, Hans," said I.

"As you will," he retorted, with a sweep of the oars which brought us under the shadow of the wharf.

Tying our boat, we hastened back to Pumpernickel's rooms, and within a half-hour of our find we were busily engaged in translating the extraordinary narrative of Captain Hammerpestle, commander of the *Gretchen B.*, a ship that, as we learned from the captain's story, was once of ill-repute, later of pleasant memory, and finally the central figure of an ocean mystery never as yet solved, though at least two hundred and fifty years had passed since she was given up for lost.

The story was in substance as follows:

II

THE TALE OF CAPTAIN HAMMERPESTLE

The end is approaching, and I, Rudolf Hammerpestle, of Bingen, third owner and captain of the ill-starred *Gretchen B.*, for-

"Over the Plum-Pudding"

merly known as the *Dutch Avenger*, will
shortly find a watery grave in sixty-eight
fathoms of the Atlantic, ninety miles west
of the rock of Gibraltar.

The *Gretchen B.* is sinking, and the
pirate ghost is at last a victor, though I
have given him a pretty fight these many
days. Had it not been for my own stu-
pidity in employing a foreign crew, all
might yet be well, and I am impelled in my
last moments, for we are sure to go to the
bottom within two hours, to write out this
story merely in the hope that it may some
day reach my fellow-men, tell them of my
horrible fate, and possibly warn them
against my errors. If I had stuck to my
own countrymen, if I had employed Hans
Stickenfurst and good old Diedrich Foutzenhickle and their like. for my officers and
crew, instead of the idiot Pat Sullivan and
his twin, Barney O'Brien, and others of
that ilk, I should now be nearing port that
I shall never reach, instead of sinking,
slowly sinking, into the mysterious depths
of the great ocean.

I have locked myself within my cabin so
as to be free from interruption, and it is

highly probable that, having tightly closed my port and calked up the door-cracks and key-hole, I shall be able to gain an extra hour for the writing of this tale even after the *Gretchen B.* has disappeared beneath the waves, to be hid forevermore from the eyes of man. When the tale is finished I shall place it within my trusty water-bottle, open the port, thrust it forth into the sea, and trust to Heaven that it may rise to the surface and ultimately make some port where it may be read and published, I devoutly hope, by some house of standing.

And now, as every story should begin at the beginning, let me go back to the time when I first took charge of the *Gretchen B.* It was five years agone, on the 7th day of May, 1635, that the *Gretchen B.* was purchased by her present owners, and I, Rudolf Hammerpestle, of Bingen, appointed her commander. It was with a light heart, a full crew, and sixty barrels of Schnitzelhammerstein claret that I set out from Bingen on the 27th day of May, 1635, for London, where the claret was to be sold to the public as medicinal port—its nutty flavor, its bouquet, and other properties

"Over the Plum-Pudding"

favoring the illusion. All went well with us until we reached the sea, when one night, after our second day on the ocean, feeling faint from the effects of the sun, for I had had a hard day of it, I tapped one of the barrels of my cargo for a taste of the claret. Understand, I was not in any sense taking away from the full measure which was due to the purchaser in London, for I intended to replace what I had taken with water— so slight in quantity, too, as not to affect the flavor appreciably. Imagine my consternation to find the liquid turned sour and thin—so thin that under no circumstances could it ever pass muster as medicinal port. I was horrified. Ours had always been an honorable firm. What was to be done? My employers' reputation was at stake. If that claret had ever been delivered at London as port they were ruined. I determined to run the *Gretchen B.* to Naples, and there dispose of my cargo as Chianti, to which, with the infusion of a little whale-oil for appearance' sake, it could be made to bear a remarkable resemblance.

This done, I retired to my cabin to reflect. What could it have been that had wrought such a change, for on leaving Bingen the wine was sweet and good? I locked my door so as to be undisturbed, for I cannot think when there are others about; but hardly had I seated myself at my table when, upon the honor of a sea-captain, a ruffianly person, noiseless as a cat, *walked through the massive oaken barrier I had but just fastened to!*

"Who—what are you?" I cried, aghast, the spectral quality of the apparition being at once manifest.

"Oh!" he retorted. "It seems to me it's more to the point for *me* to ask that question. You are the interloper."

"It is my cabin," I said, indignantly.

"Oh, is it?" he sneered. "Since when?"

"Since the seventh day of May," I replied. "I am the commander of this craft."

"Pooh!" said he, harshly. "Do you know who I am?"

"I've asked you once," said I, trying hard to appear calm and sarcastic.

"Well, I almost hate to tell you," he said, throwing off his coat, whereon I was filled with consternation to observe that his belt held four wicked-looking blunderbusses and six cutlasses of razor edge. "You're not a bad fellow, and your hair will turn white when I tell you; but since you ask, so be it. Your hair be upon your own head. *I am the ghost of Wouter von Rotterdaam!*"

"You?" I cried, clutching wildly at my locks, not to keep them from turning white, of course, but to steady my nerves, for in the name I recognized that of one of the most successful pirates, and the bloodiest in his way.

"Ay, I!" he replied, impressively.

"But—who—what do you here on board the *Gretchen B.?*" I cried.

"*Gretchen* nothing," he said. "This is the *Dutch Avenger*, upon which, after her capture, six months ago, I was hanged, and which, my dear Hammerpestle, I shall haunt till she fills her destiny, which is *there!*"

The word "there" was pronounced in sepulchral tones, and with Von Rotterdaam's forefinger pointed downward. I shivered from top to toe, but quickly recovered.

"If *I* cannot have the *Dutch Avenger*, at least none other shall have her," he added.

"You are mistaken, Mr. von Rotterdaam," I said, politely. "You have taken the wrong boat, sir. This is not the *Dutch Avenger*, but the *Gretchen B.*, of Bingen."

"She has not always been the *Gretchen B.*, of Bingen," he replied.

"I know that, my dear sir," I observed, "but her previous name was the *Anneke van der Q.*"

"*Anneke van der* bosh!" he ejaculated, with a laugh. "That is what they told you, and you swallowed the bait. They knew precious well your people wouldn't buy her if they had ever guessed she'd once been the terror of the seas as the *Dutch Avenger* of everywhere, the ubiquitous ranger of the deep, Captain Wouter von Rotterdaam, better known as the Throat-Cutter of the Caribbees."

"Is that the truth?" I replied.

"As a pirate, I scorn lies," he answered. "We don't need 'em in our business. Get your carpenter to plane off the name on her stern and see!" and even as he spoke he disappeared, fading away through the closed door.

I was nearly prostrated by the revelation, but, hoping for disproof, I rushed up on

deck, summoned the carpenter, and ordered
the name *Gretchen B.* planed off the stern.
Alas! there beneath the innocent letters
lay the horrid proof of the truth of the
spectre's story, the words *Dutch Avenger,*
flanked on either side by skull and cross-
bones.

Again I sought my room, to recover, and
to my added distress Von Rotterdaam had
returned, an ugly look on his face.

"You've changed your course!" he said,
savagely.

"I know it," said I. "My cargo is spoiled
for the original market. I am taking it
where it is salable."

He was very wroth.

"I was not aware that you were so clever
a man," said he, after a moment, calming
down. "I perceive that my attempt to ruin
you interlopers at the outset is to be attended
with some difficulty. You have individual
resources upon which I had not counted."

"Ah!" said I. "It was you who turned
the claret sour?"

"It was," he replied—"as a part of my
revenge. And, mark you, Captain Hammerpestle, no cargo shall ever reach its

The Loss of the "Gretchen B."

destination unspoiled while I have a bit of the old spook left in me. Where are we bound now?"

"To Naples," said I, incautiously, and I further foolishly unfolded my plan to dispose of the cargo as Chianti.

"See here, captain," he said, pleadingly, "give up this honest seafaring business and come out as a pirate, won't you? You're too clever a chap to be honest. Keep the *Dutch Avenger* going as a terror, and, by Jingo, sir, I'll stand by you to the last."

My answer was the lighting of a sulphur candle in the hope of exorcising him, and, going on deck, I ordered the name *Gretchen B.* restored, merely to emphasize my determination to have no part in his foul schemes of piracy.

I must now pause in my narrative for a moment, and see how far we have settled in the water. It may be I shall have to write somewhat less in detail so as to finish the tale before I am destroyed by the inrush of the sea.

It is as I feared. The rippling surface of the ocean is already lapping the lower edge

"Over the Plum-Pudding"

of my circular port window, and one or two drops have leaked within. It will not be long, I fear, before the water from below will burst the decks and dash against my door, when, of course, we shall sink the more rapidly, but if the walls of my cabin, and they are unquestionably strong, Von Rotterdaam having had them made bullet-proof, of wrought-iron—if these can withstand the pressure of the water for a half-hour after we are submerged, I am quite confident I can finish the story in time to bottle it up and launch it safely through the port.

After many days of difficulty we passed the Strait of Gibraltar, and on the 18th of July were safely anchored in the Bay of Naples, where I sold the claret, which Von Rotterdaam had changed into water, as the latest mineral product of the Schnitzelhammerstein Spa.

But from the hour of my refusal to compromise with my honor and become the successor and partner of Von Rotterdaam in the profession of piracy we had trouble on board.

The Loss of the "Gretchen B."

Letting my cargo alone, he introduced a system of haunting my crew, so that at the end of several years not a German-speaking sailor was anxious to ship with me, except at ruinously high wages. I found some, but not many, and finally I was reduced to the followers of the two men I have already mentioned—Hans Stickenfurst and Diedrich Foutzenhickle—men who had never known fear, and who, when Von Rotterdaam haunted them, merely laughed and blew the vile-smelling smoke from their pipes into his face. But while the pirate ghost was powerless to fill the men with fear, he did arouse a great interest in the stories of his booty which he told. Night after night, lying in my cabin, I could hear him in the forecastle telling them tales of his prowess, and giving forth vague hints as to where vast treasure was hid which might become theirs if only I would come around and become his successor. The night we entered port I overheard a compact made between them, that on the next outward voyage they would first reason with me and persuade me, if possible, to accept his proposition, and, failing in that, to seize the ship, put me in the

long-boat, turn me adrift, and place themselves subject to Von Rotterdaam's orders.

That was a year ago. Since then, until
this ill-fated voyage (by-the-way, as I look
up the water is clear over the port window,
and is beginning to trickle in under the
door, so I must again hasten)—until this
ill-fated voyage, I was not again on the
sea, and having in mind the threats of my
crew, which they do not even now know that
I overheard, I secured for this voyage the
crew of an Irish bark, discharging all my
previous men.

"I will at least have men who do not
understand Dutch or German," I thought,
"and for this voyage shall be comparatively
safe. To insure against a possible turning
adrift in the long-boat, I shall likewise sail
without it."

Alas for all my expectations! While
neither Sullivan nor O'Brien, as I had supposed, was acquainted with the native
tongue of Von Rotterdaam, that talented
ghost could speak English with as fine
a brogue as ever gilded speech; and, worse
than this, Sullivan, the carpenter, was a
flyaway fool. Genial, full of good stories,

and an excellent carpenter (the deck beneath my feet is bulging upward), he was absolutely without foresight, and it is to him I owe my present plight.

It happened this afternoon. The day had been absolutely calm and still. Not a ripple on the sea, not a breath of wind to stir even the frayed hemp in the rigging, and yet down, down, down we are sinking, *for Sullivan has sawed a hole in our bottom big enough to let a man through!*

I didn't suppose he would do it, but he has; and because last night while he and Rafferty, my second mate, were smoking in the forecastle, Von Rotterdaam's spirit rose up before them, and, arousing their cupidity, led them astray.

"For the love of the shaints!" cried Rafferty, as the ghost appeared, "phwat are you?"

Rotterdaam replied, "A spherit of the poirate Von Rotterdaam; and here where I stand, directly below me, in five fathoms of water, lies a million in treasure."

"Go on!" cried Rafferty.

"'Tis true," retorted Von Rotterdaam. "And if at noon to-morrow you will cut

241

away cnough of the ship's bottom to let yourselves through the hole, with a rope tied about you so that you can be hauled back again, it will be yours."

"Blame good pay for a shwim," said Sullivan. "A million phwat—pounds or francs, sorr? They's some difference betune the two."

"Exactly," returned Von Rotterdaam. "And they're pounds sterling, ingots of gold, and priceless jewels."

"Phwy don't yees tell the ould man?" asked Rafferty, referring to me.

"Because," replied Von Rotterdaam, "he would keep it all for himself. You gentlemen, I am sure, will divide it justly among all."

"Thrue for youse," said Sullivan, with a laugh. "And phwere do you come in?"

"I have no further use for dross," replied Von Rotterdaam; and I judge that at that moment he faded from their sight, for almost immediately he appeared in my cabin. I was tired and irritated, so I said nothing, pretending to be asleep, never for an instant believing that Sullivan would do so foolish a thing.

The Loss of the "Gretchen B."

"He doesn't ever think of consequences; but he's not such an ass as to cut a hole a yard square in the bottom of this ship," I said to myself; and then, worn out, I really slept. How it happened I do not know; possibly that infernal ghost in some manner drugged me; but it was not until five minutes after midday, just three hours ago, that I awoke, and my heart stood still as I heard the action of a saw deep down in the hold.

"Heavens!" I cried, starting up. "The idiot's at it!"

A deep, baleful laugh greeted the remark. It was from Von Rotterdaam.

"He is! And I am revenged!" he said, in tones which seemed to come from the centre of the earth, and then he vanished —I hope, forever.

I rushed madly out and called for Sullivan, but the only answer was the grating of the saw's teeth. (Dear me! how dark it is getting! I must really not linger with details.) My only answer was the grating of the saw's teeth upon the bottom of my devoted vessel. Shrieking, I clambered down into the hold, but too late. Just as I got there the yard square of planking was

243

burst in by the waters, and the vessel was doomed.

"Well, captain," I said to myself, a great calm coming over my soul, "it's all up with you; now think of others. Those at home, not hearing from you, will be worried. Go to your cabin, and, like a dutiful man, make your report."

This I have done, and this narrative is my report. I hope it will reach its destination in safety, and that the world may yet learn that in the hour of peril, which has but one conclusion, I have been faithful and calm.

It is now the 16th day of June, 1640. I shall never see the 17th, and I am resigned to my fate. And now for the bottle . . . now for the cork . . . Blithering cyclones! the door is cracking open . . . and now—one—two—three—to open the port . . . wait. I must put in one final P.S. In case this story ever reaches the land, will the finder kindly be careful in correcting the proof and see that my name is spelled correctly? There is just a moment in which to write it plainly—RUDOLF— with an F, mark you, not a PH, and HAM-

The Loss of the "Gretchen B."

MERPESTLE with two M's. And so—
the port . . .

There the story ends, and here it is for the
world to see. What followed Captain Hammerpestle's last word we can only surmise.
Pumpernickel and I have been faithful to
the trust unwittingly committed to our care
by one who has been dead for a trifle over
two hundred and sixty years. We have
only to add that those who do not believe
that the story is true can see the water-
bottle at the home of Herr Pumpernickel
at Schnitzelhammerstein-on-the-Zugvitz at
any time; but as for the manuscript and
the ghost of the pirate Von Rotterdaam,
we do not know where they are. The latter
we have ourselves never seen, and the former
was, as usual, mislaid by the talented young
person who undertook to make a type-written
copy of it for us a few days after our discovery.

THE END

Reprint Publishing

FOR PEOPLE WHO GO FOR ORIGINALS.

This book is a facsimile reprint of the original edition. The term refers to the facsimile with an original in size and design exactly matching simulation as photographic or scanned reproduction.

Facsimile editions offer us the chance to join in the library of historical, cultural and scientific history of mankind, and to rediscover.

The books of the facsimile edition may have marks, notations and other marginalia and pages with errors contained in the original volume. These traces of the past refers to the historical journey that has covered the book.

ISBN 978-3-95940-059-6

Facsimile reprint of the original edition
Copyright © 2015 Reprint Publishing
All rights reserved.

Made in Germany

www.reprintpublishing.com